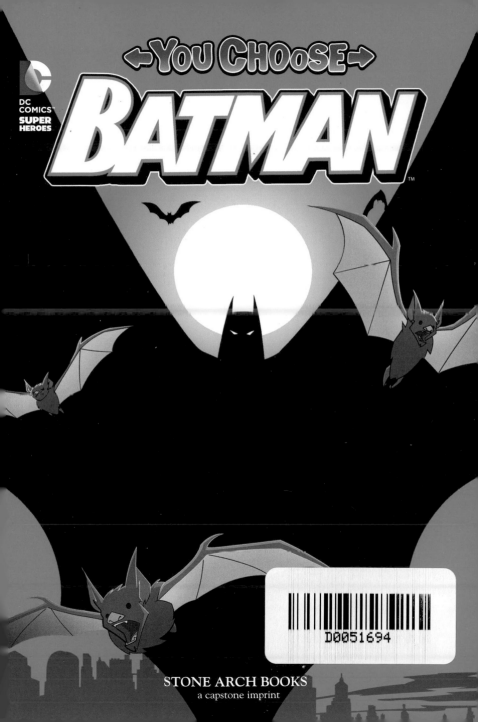

← YOU CHOOSE →

BATMAN ™

STONE ARCH BOOKS
a capstone imprint

D0051694

You Choose Stories: Batman
is published by Stone Arch Books,
A Capstone Imprint
1710 Roe Crest Drive
North Mankato, Minnesota 56003
www.capstonepub.com

STAR34129

Cataloging-in-Publication Data is available
on the Library of Congress website.
ISBN: 978-1-4965-0528-6 (library binding)
ISBN: 978-1-4965-0530-9 (paperback)
ISBN: 978-1-4965-2305-1 (eBook)

Summary: A wave of crime has hit Gotham City
and the ferocious Bane is behind the spree.
With your help, Batman will solve the puzzle of
the Super-Villain Smackdown!

Printed in Canada.
042015      008825FRF15

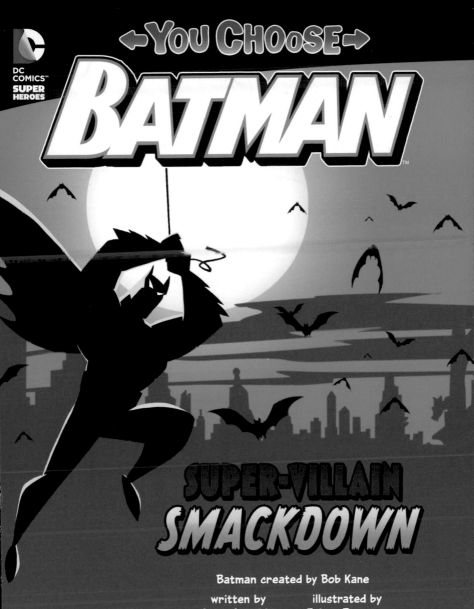

# YOU CHOOSE

# BATMAN™

DC COMICS™
SUPER HEROES

# SUPER-VILLAIN SMACKDOWN

Batman created by Bob Kane

written by
**John Sazaklis**

illustrated by
**Ethen Beavers**

A wave of crime has hit Gotham City, and the ferocious Bane is behind the spree. With your help, Batman will solve the puzzle of the *Super-Villain Smackdown*!

Follow the directions at the bottom of each page. The choices YOU make will change the outcome of the story. After you finish one path, go back and read the others for more Batman adventures!

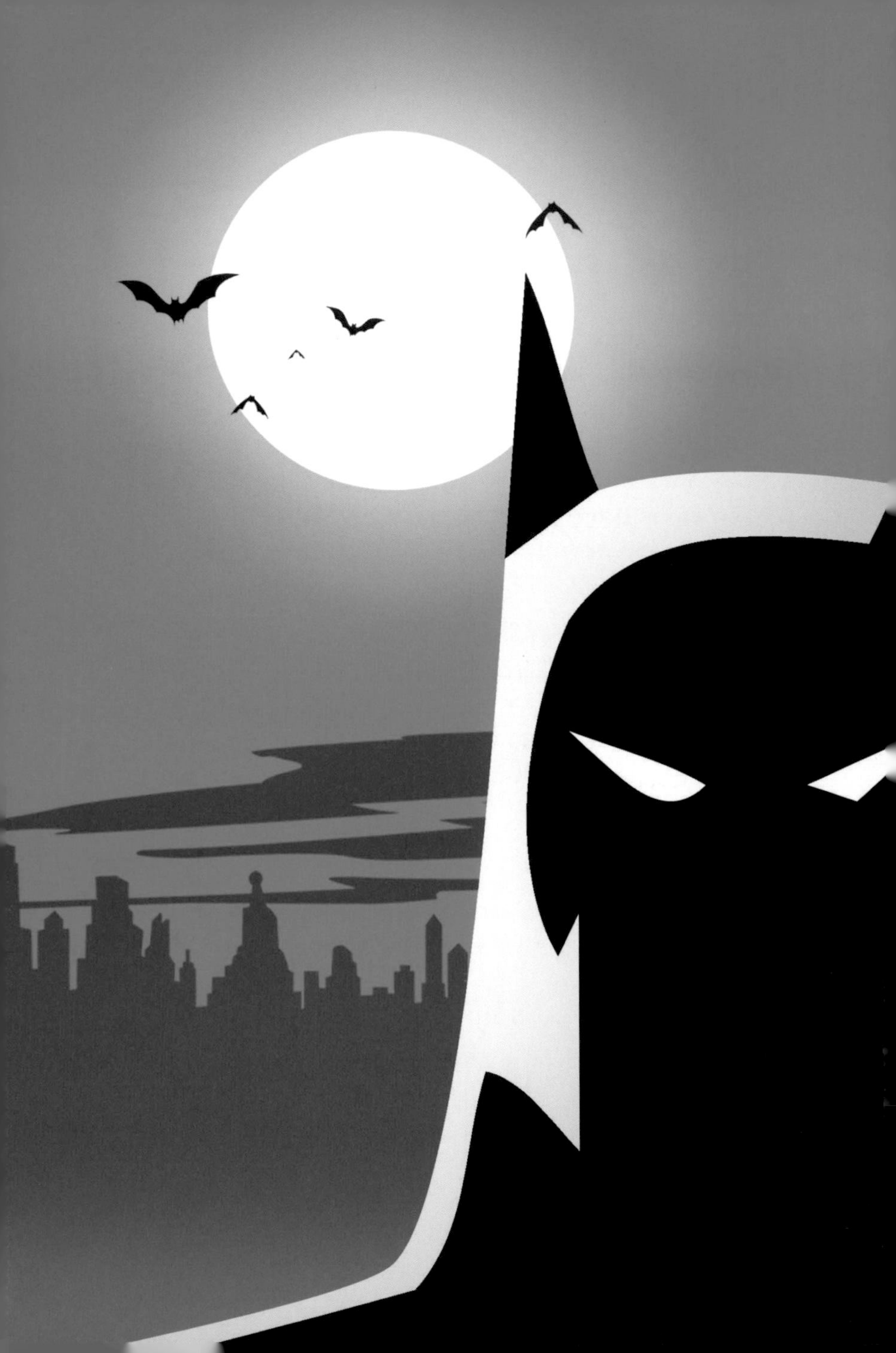

"See ya, wouldn't want to be ya!" hollers the
Joker as he runs across the rooftop of the Laffco
Toy Factory. He straps himself into a turbo-
powered jetpack while Batman sprints after him.

Once the hero is within reaching distance, the
Joker activates his jetpack and launches himself
into the air. *FWOOOSH!*

"It's been a blast, Batman! HA HA HA!"
cackles the Clown Prince of Crime.

Batman stops short and skids across the
ledge. Below him is a two-hundred-foot drop. He
narrows his eyes to focus on the fleeing foe.

The Joker waves his arms, sticks out his
tongue, and blows a raspberry. *FFBBBLT!*

"We'll see who has the last laugh, Joker,"
Batman says to himself. Then he reaches into his
Utility Belt.

Turn the page.

Batman pulls out his grapnel gun. He takes aim and presses the trigger. The compressed air within shoots out a long Kevlar cable with a titanium hook at the end. The hook loops itself around the Joker's foot, snaring him.

Batman leaps off the roof, using his weight to pull the villain down.

"Hey!" shouts the Joker. "No free rides!"

As the Dark Knight falls from the top of the factory, his cape billows out behind him like a hang glider. This decreases his speed, and he lands gently next to the Batmobile in the alley behind Laffco.

"Your joyride is over, Joker," Batman says. He pulls hard on the cable, forcing the criminal clown out of the air.

"Mayday! Mayday!" screams the Joker. His jetpack is sputtering and coughing. "Looks like I'm coming in for a crash landing!"

**SMASH!**

Turn to page 10.

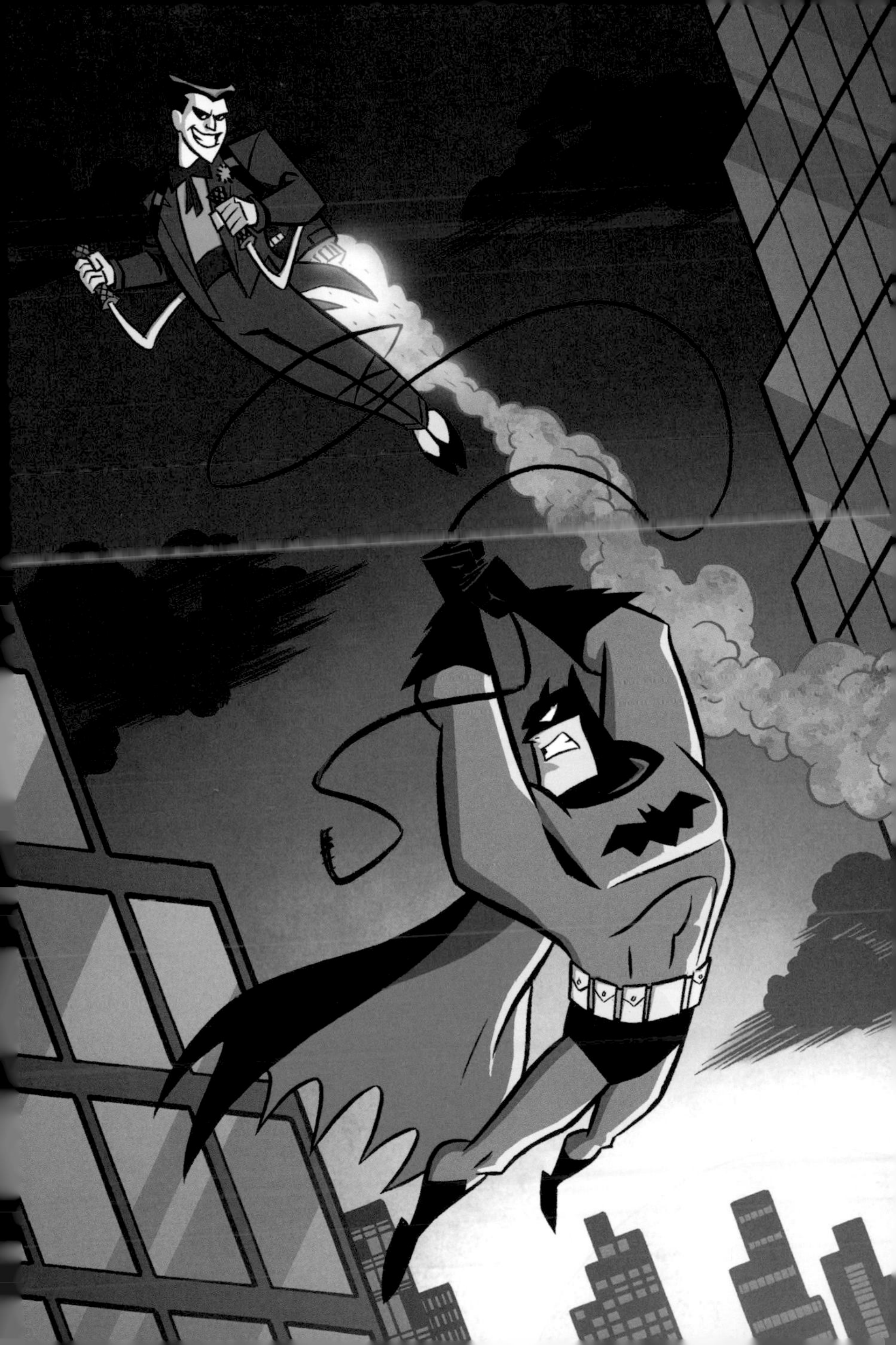

The Joker slams onto the hood of the Batmobile. He groans and goes limp.

Batman loads the unconscious prankster into the high-tech vehicle, strapping him into the passenger seat.

Soon, the Caped Crusader and his cargo are heading out of the city and up an isolated road to a foreboding building on a hilltop. The sign on the wrought iron gate reads ARKHAM ASYLUM. This sanitarium is home for the criminally insane, and where Gotham City's most dangerous denizens of society come for rehabilitation.

Batman drags the Joker inside. "Got room for one more?" he says to Dr. Arkham.

Soon after, Batman heads back to the Batcave located discreetly beneath Wayne Manor, the residence of billionaire Bruce Wayne — Batman's alter ego. Gotham City's masked protector is also one of its richest and most upstanding citizens!

Once inside the cave, Batman exits the Batmobile and is greeted by Alfred Pennyworth, his loyal butler.

The prim and proper Englishman is carrying a silver serving tray with a delicious sandwich and a cold glass of juice.

"Eat up, Master Bruce," he advises. "Your night has just begun."

Bruce changes out of his Batman gear and sits down in the study to eat.

Just as he finishes, the doorbell rings.

Alfred opens the front door to greet Vicki Vale, star journalist for the Gotham News Network. She is wearing a glittering gown, and her hair and makeup are expertly styled.

"Good evening, Ms. Vale," Alfred says with a bow. "Do come in. Master Bruce will be a few minutes late, I'm afraid."

"Nonsense," laughs a voice. "I could never keep a lady waiting!"

Alfred and Vicki turn to see Bruce, gleaming, groomed, and in a perfectly tailored tuxedo, standing at the top of the stairs.

Turn the page.

"Well, you sure know how to make an entrance," Vicki says as Bruce leans down to kiss her hand.

"You look radiant," he replies. "Shall we?"

The pair gets into Bruce's town car, and Alfred drives them to Gotham Square Garden.

Upon arrival, Bruce and Vicki find the sporting arena crowded by photographers. A large digital billboard reads: GOTHAM CITY GLADIATORS: ONE NIGHT ONLY!

The couple finds their seats and settles in to watch the first bout of celebrity wrestlers.

"What an exciting event," Bruce whispers.

"Oh, I think it's all fake," Vicki replies.

Finally, it's time for the main attraction: Stephen "Bruiser" Brown versus Matthew "Crusher" Cody! The announcer calls for the fight to begin, but neither of the wrestlers appears. A referee rushes over and whispers something in the announcer's ear.

Suddenly, the Bat-Signal lights up the night sky. The spectators see it through the glass dome in the ceiling and gasp. Police Commissioner Gordon is calling Batman for help.

If Bruce excuses himself to change into Batman, turn to page 14.

If Bruce ignores the signal so as not to reveal his secret identity, turn to page 24.

"The Bat-Signal!" Vicki exclaims. "Maybe we'll see Batman in action!"

Bruce walks into the aisle, pretending to get a better look. He purposefully bumps into the concessions server as she walks by. Soda and popcorn spill all over his tuxedo.

"Oops, clumsy me!" Bruce says. "I'm so embarrassed. Pardon me, Vicki. I must get to a dry cleaner at once." He hurries out of the arena before his date can protest. "I'll call you!" he shouts over his shoulder.

The billionaire ducks out the back entrance into the alley behind the arena. As expected, Alfred is already there with the town car.

Silently, Bruce enters the backseat. Alfred presses a button on the dashboard that locks the doors and tints the windows black. No one can see in or out. Bruce begins his transformation into Batman.

"Shall I contact the Batmobile or the Batplane via remote control, sir?" the butler asks.

"No need," Bruce replies. "Police headquarters are only a few blocks away. I'll get there the old-fashioned way."

"Yes, of course," Alfred replies.

Moments later, the sunroof slides open. A grappling hook launches onto the top ledge of a nearby building. As the cable recoils, the Dark Knight dramatically emerges from the town car.

Alfred drives away as Batman sails upward over the city skyline.

On the rooftop of police headquarters, Commissioner Gordon awaits next to the Bat-Signal. He senses a slight flutter behind him and turns around. Batman is perched on the ledge like a gargoyle.

Gordon gasps. "I'll never get used to that."

"What have we got?" Batman asks.

Commissioner Gordon tells the Caped Crusader that Stephen "Bruiser" Brown's manager called, claiming that the wrestler had gone missing.

Turn the page.

"He never showed up for his big fight at the Garden tonight," continues Gordon. "He's not answering his phone, and he's not at his apartment."

"Technically, not enough time has passed to declare him a missing person," Batman states.

"Correct, but his celebrity status makes this a high-profile case," replies the Commissioner. "No ransom demands have been made yet, but we can't rule out kidnapping."

The Commissioner hands Batman a small slip of paper. "That's Bruiser's address," he says. "You have the reputation of being the World's Greatest Detective. See if you can find any clues that will help us solve this mystery."

Suddenly, the roof door bursts open. A young policeman runs toward the Commissioner.

"Sir, we have a situation," he pants.

"What is it, Officer Henry?" asks the Commissioner.

"There has been a break-in at the First National Bank. The officers on call say it's nothing they've ever dealt with before!"

"I doubt this is a coincidence," Batman says.

The voice startles Officer Henry. "Is that who I think it is?" he asks.

As his eyes adjust, they make out a pointy-eared silhouette against the full moon. In a split second, it's gone.

"No comment," replies Commissioner Gordon.

If Batman goes to the bank to help the police, turn to page 18.
If he goes to Bruiser's apartment to search for clues, turn to page 53.

Moments later, Batman lands across from the First National Bank. He surveys the situation with his high-tech binoculars. The police force on hand has barricaded the perimeter with their cruisers.

A GNN van pulls up and two passengers disembark: Vicki Vale and her camerawoman. They've arrived to cover the breaking news story.

Outside the bank stands a band of thugs in battle gear blocking the building's entrance. Through the large glass doors, Batman sees a hulking brute in a black mask approach the vault. With muscles bulging, the bank robber rips the steel vault door off its hinges as if he were opening a tin can and then tosses it aside.

### CLANG!

Batman formulates a plan in his head.

If Batman springs into action, turn to page 20.
If Batman waits to see what happens next, turn to page 41.

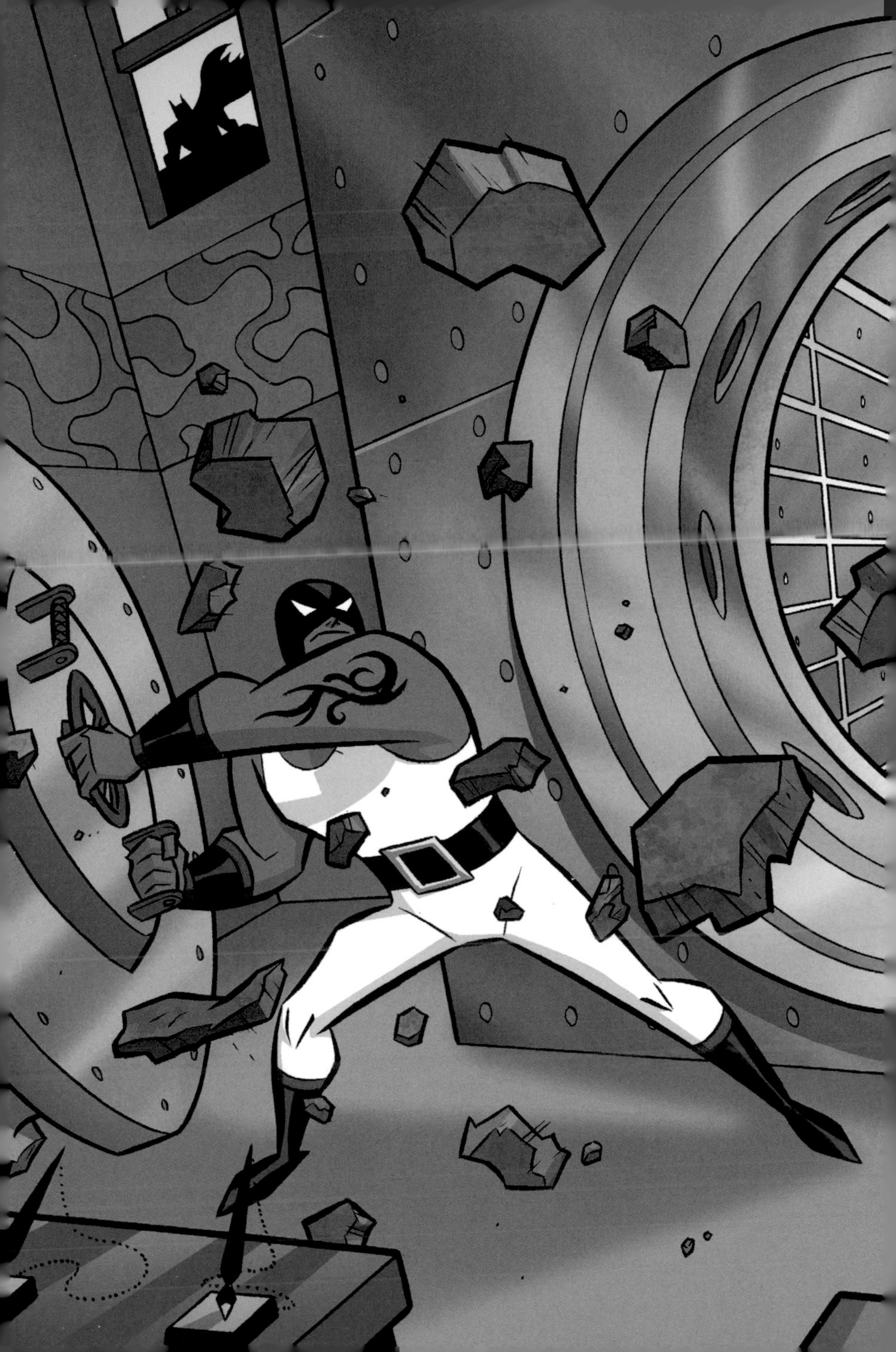

Taking a running start, Batman leaps onto the nearest police car and somersaults toward the bank, simultaneously throwing gas pellets from his Utility Belt. The miniature capsules explode upon impact, releasing thick clouds of smoke and disorienting the thugs. *FSSSSSSS!*

Batman is an expert of martial arts techniques. With precision and speed, he unleashes a flurry of devastating blows that render the thugs unconscious.

### *POW! WHAP! THWACK!*

When the smoke clears, the henchmen lie in a pile at his feet. Batman turns his attention to the massive man-mountain who is stuffing his satchel with money from inside the vault.

"Your withdrawal has been denied," the Dark Knight says.

The bandit does not seem to hear or notice Batman. The hero pulls out a Batarang and hurls it. The bladed projectile tears the bottom of the satchel, and all the loot pours out. This time, the bandit notices.

He whirls to face Batman and snarls.
**"GRRRRR!"** Then he charges at the Dark
Knight like a bull.

Batman quickly sidesteps and jumps onto the
bank robber's back. With one deft movement, the
Dark Knight removes the bandit's mask . . . and
sees his face.

It's Bruiser!

The wrestler thrashes, shaking Batman off his
back.

The hero tries to reason with him, but Bruiser
seems to be in a trance. His eyes are wide, his
jaw is clenched, and the muscles in his neck
are tense enough to snap. With a ferocious roar,
Bruiser lunges toward Batman.

If Batman fights back, turn to page 22.
If Batman sprays Bruiser with sleeping gas, turn to page 79.

Batman braces himself for Bruiser's attack. The fighter tackles the Caped Crusader to the ground. Luckily, Batman's body armor absorbs most of the hit.

Bruiser rears back to head-butt Batman, but the hero judo chops him in the throat. The momentary distraction gives Batman enough time to roll away. Bruiser's boot comes crashing down on the same location where Batman lay seconds earlier. There are cracks in the marble floor tiles from the impact.

"MUST CRUSH BAT!" Bruiser shouts.

Batman hurls his Batrope up at the ceiling and swings over the wrestler. He climbs onto a nearby column.

*Clearly, someone smart and devious is behind Bruiser's behavior,* Batman thinks to himself. *And these symptoms are so familiar, I know exactly who it is.*

Before Batman can react, a blinding spotlight floods the bank lobby. A voice echoes through a megaphone.

"FREEZE! This is Police Commissioner Gordon. Stephen Brown, you are under arrest. I order you to stand down."

Two police officers barge into the bank.

"Get back!" Batman yells at them.

Bruiser roars with rage and punches a nearby column before he runs out the back door. The sheer force of his strength causes the concrete structure to crack and crumble.

Batman swings forward and kicks the policemen out of harm's way. The column collapses, burying the hero under a pile of rubble. *CRASH!*

Digging his way through the debris, the Dark Knight vows that he and Bruiser will cross paths again.

**THE END**

To follow another path, turn to page 13.

Bruce ignores the Bat-Signal but discreetly reaches into the pocket of his blazer. There is a small remote control device in there. He presses a button and sends a signal back to the Batcave. Inside the dark cavern, the Batplane roars to life.

Suddenly, the lights go out, startling the crowd. Then the enormous digital screen over the ring turns on. A masked man appears in extreme close-up.

"Ladies and gentlemen," bellows a voice through the surround sound system. "I AM BANE! To see a real match, tune in tomorrow night. Same time, same place! I challenge Batman to fight me here in this very arena to prove once and for all that *I* am the ultimate Gotham City Gladiator."

Turn to page 26.

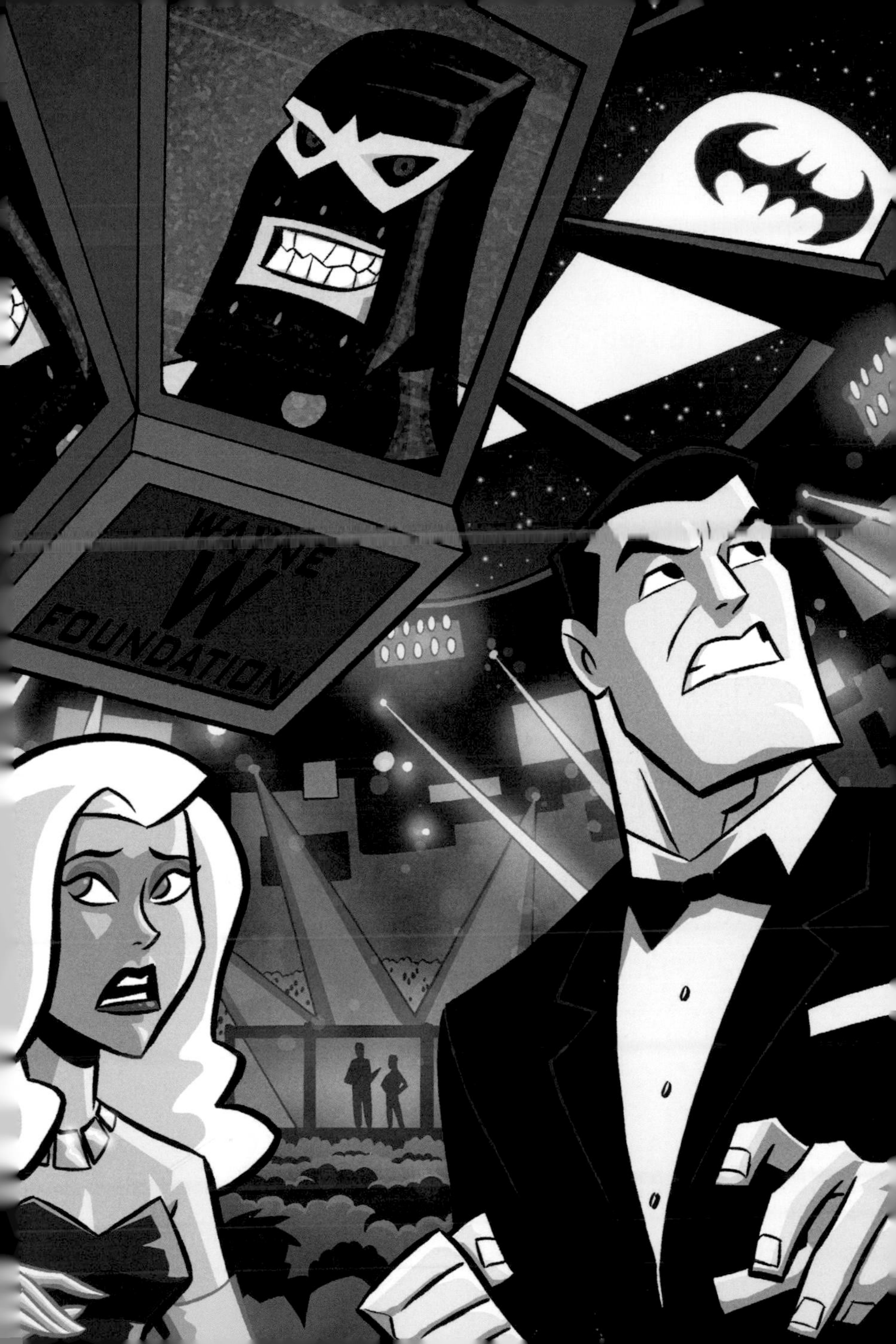
W
FOUNDATION

Just as suddenly, the screen goes black and the lights return. All traces of Bane are gone. The spectators are abuzz with excitement and fear.

*It's time to act,* Bruce thinks. He turns to excuse himself, but Vicki is already on her feet.

"Listen, Bruce," she says, putting on her coat. "You're a great date, but I have to run. This is big news!"

Vicki disappears in the crowd, and Bruce wastes no time running to a secluded janitor's closet. Quickly, he rips off his tuxedo to reveal the Batsuit. Then he pulls the cowl over his head and bounds up the emergency staircase to the arena's roof. As expected, the autopiloted Batplane is already there.

"Time to move," Batman says.

If Batman tracks Bane to his broadcasting location, turn to page 27.

If Batman answers the Bat-Signal and goes to police headquarters, turn to page 91.

Batman climbs into the sleek and silent Batplane and activates the console. He tracks the frequency of the signal used for Bane's broadcast. The screen blips and beeps while it searches. In the meantime, Batman pulls up all the information he has logged in the Batcomputer about Bane.

Bane was once an inmate at the Peña Duro prison. He became the test subject of a government project to create superpowered soldiers and was given a steroid called Venom.

The test was a success, and Bane became a chemically boosted brawler with enhanced endurance and the strength to punch through solid brick! He stole the Venom formula and escaped the prison.

When news of Bane's amazing abilities spread through Gotham City's criminal underworld, the gangster Rupert Thorne paid a large sum of money to use those very talents. Rupert hired Bane to eliminate the Caped Crusader himself — Batman!

Turn the page.

Thorne's wicked plot was foiled when Batman proved to be too great an adversary for Bane. Now the villain wanted revenge against the hero.

Bane pumps the Venom directly into his head from a dispenser in his glove that courses through a tube attached to the back of his mask. That way, he is always at the ready if he ever confronts Batman. This time, he made the first move by calling him out on national television.

**BEEP! BEEP!** The Batcomputer gets a reading on Bane's location. The signal is coming from the northwest quadrant of the city. There is only one news media studio in that area — GNN.

"Hey, Batman!" crackles a voice. Then a face appears on the dashboard next to the radar screen. It belongs to Robin, the Boy Wonder — junior detective, acrobat, and Batman's sidekick.

"I heard about what happened at the Garden. The Internet is blowing up with people commenting about who will win in a fight between you and Bane. Just so you know, you have my vote!"

"Bane's extreme behavior is very serious," Batman states. "I'm headed to the GNN TV station to pull the plug on this situation. Over and out."

Turn to page 31.

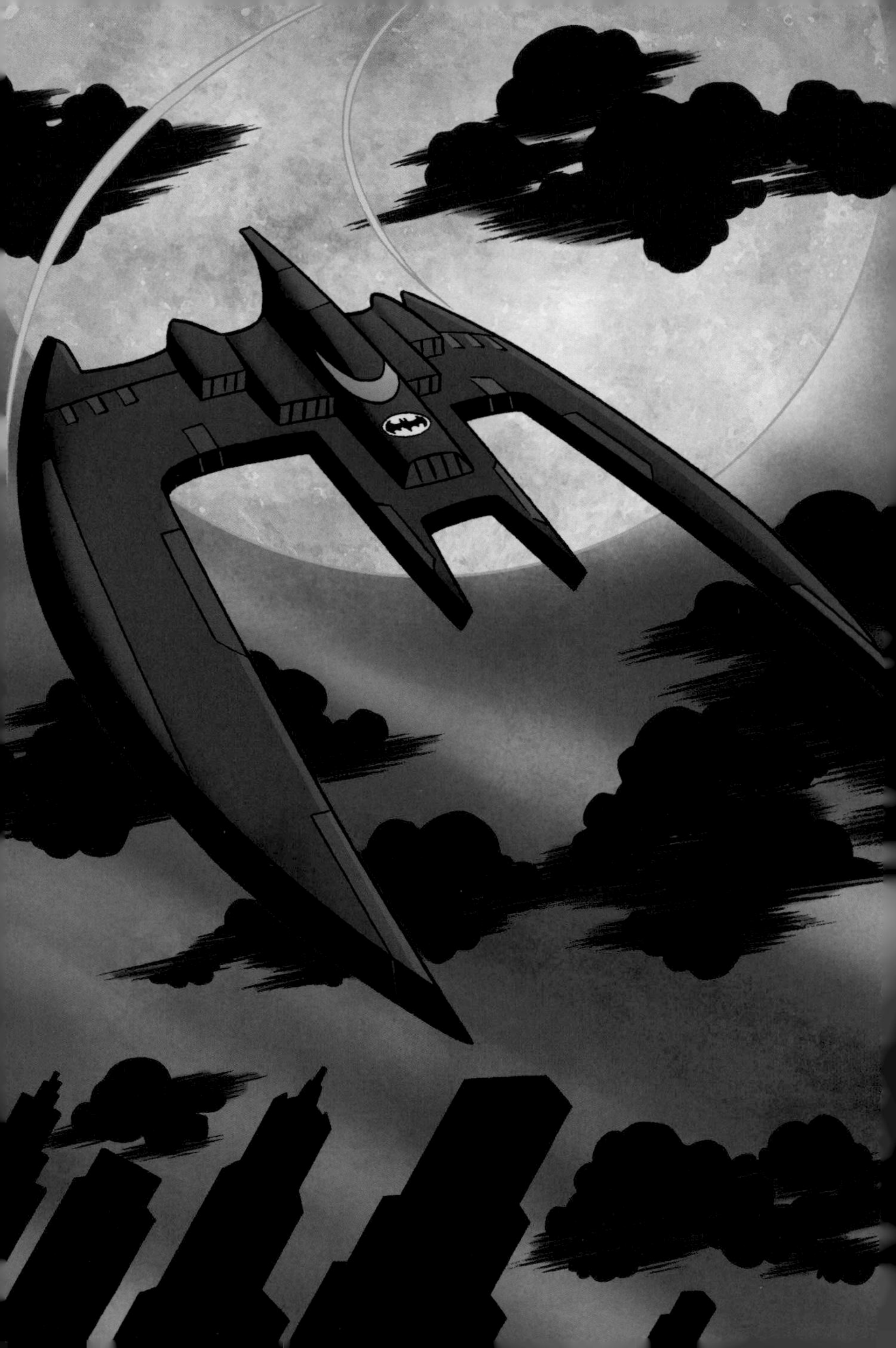

Batman pilots the Batplane through the concrete jungle that is Gotham City. Weaving expertly in and out of skyscrapers, the hero finally arrives above GNN Studio.

The Batplane lands on the roof, and Batman exits. The main news studio is located on the top floor of the building. At this hour, the studio should be unoccupied and shut down. But there is light streaming up from the skylight.

Batman looks down to see Bane and his thugs prepping the cameras for another announcement. They are oblivious to his presence. To his right, Batman finds a large air duct that leads into the building's heating and cooling system.

*These guys are sitting ducks,* Batman thinks to himself. *They won't know what hit them.*

If Batman goes through the vent for a silent approach, turn to page 32.

If he crashes through the skylight, turn to page 74.

Batman decides to take the stealthy route through the large air duct. He reaches into his Utility Belt and removes a small penlight to illuminate the narrow passageway. Batman climbs down and slowly crawls over the stage set.

Luckily, Bane's booming voice echoes through the vent — guiding the Dark Knight directly above him. Batman overhears Bane's plot.

"This powerful young man shows promising potential," Bane says. "Bruiser has certainly made the perfect candidate for my new and improved batch of Venom. Just wait until Gotham City gets a load of him!"

"What about Batman?" asks one of the thugs.

"Bah! Once that pointy-eared pipsqueak undoubtedly accepts my challenge, he'll be in for a big, bad surprise! Ha, ha, hah!"

Meanwhile, another one of Bane's thugs is standing in the main booth across from the set. He is monitoring the building's security cameras. Suddenly, he sees a figure walking down the hall toward the newsroom.

"Hey, boss!" he hollers. "There's someone coming this way. It's that news lady, Vicki Vale!"

"Hmm," Bane muses. "It appears Ms. Vale is putting in some overtime. Excellent. Let's give her a grand tale to tell!"

Batman hears Vicki's high heels clacking against the linoleum floor. She is fast approaching the room. The Caped Crusader fears that the journalist is putting herself in danger without knowing it.

If Batman crawls back to warn Vicki, turn to page 34.
If he strikes Bane and his men now, turn to page 74.

Batman knows that Vicki's safety is more important and turns to crawl back. As he does so, the rickety duct panels loosen and suddenly collapse under Batman's weight. **CRASH!**

Batman falls through the ceiling in a shower of debris. A thick cloud of plaster and drywall fills the air. His presence is no longer a secret.

"Welcome, Batman!" Bane bellows. "You couldn't wait to face me! This wasn't the venue I had planned, but I am welcome to oblige you with a preview of tomorrow's main event."

The villain turns to his thugs and orders, "Get him, boys!"

The two thugs nearest the desk attack first. Batman jumps high, extends both legs, and kicks the men square in the chest. They tumble backward and fall hard.

Back on his feet, Batman senses three thugs heading toward him from behind. He spins in a circle and flaps his cape across their faces. **WHAP!** Then he drops low and sweep kicks the first thug.

Batman moves on to the second thug and delivers a shattering uppercut. The second thug sails straight onto the third, and they land in a crumpled heap. *THUD!*

Curious about the loud commotion, Vicki enters the room. She gasps at the sight.

"Another uninvited guest," Bane exclaims as he grabs her wrist. "Now to become a lovely hostage!"

If Batman trades himself for Vicki, turn to page 36.
If Batman attacks Bane, turn to page 86.

"Let me go, you bloated brute!" Vicki screams.

Bane laughs and pulls her closer.

"What a delicate little flower," he sneers. "I wouldn't want you to wilt too soon."

"Enough!" Batman shouts. "Let her go and take me instead." He holds his hands up to show he is not a threat anymore.

Bane nods and instructs his men to grab Batman. They pin his arms back and hold him tight.

"A noble gesture, Caped Crusader," Bane says. "I'll let her go, but not too far." Bane hands Vicki over to a nearby henchman.

The villain then approaches the hero. "You're making this too easy, Batman. Let's see how powerful you are when you're not hiding behind that foolish mask!"

Bane reaches to remove Batman's cowl when all of a sudden —

**SKEESH!**

A small figure smashes through the skylight. His bright yellow cape billows behind him as he dives through the shower of falling glass.

"ROBIN!" shouts Bane.

"Mind if I crash this party?" asks the Boy Wonder.

He lands behind the thugs holding Batman and knocks their heads together. **BONK!**

"Not at all," Batman replies, massaging his arms. "Thanks for dropping by." Then he whirls around and grabs Bane by the shirt. Before the villain can react, Batman head-butts him hard.

**CRUNCH!**

"By doze!" Bane hollers, clutching his nose.

"For your information, Bane," Batman says, "this 'foolish' mask is also made of a very strong carbon-fiber composite."

Turn to page 39.

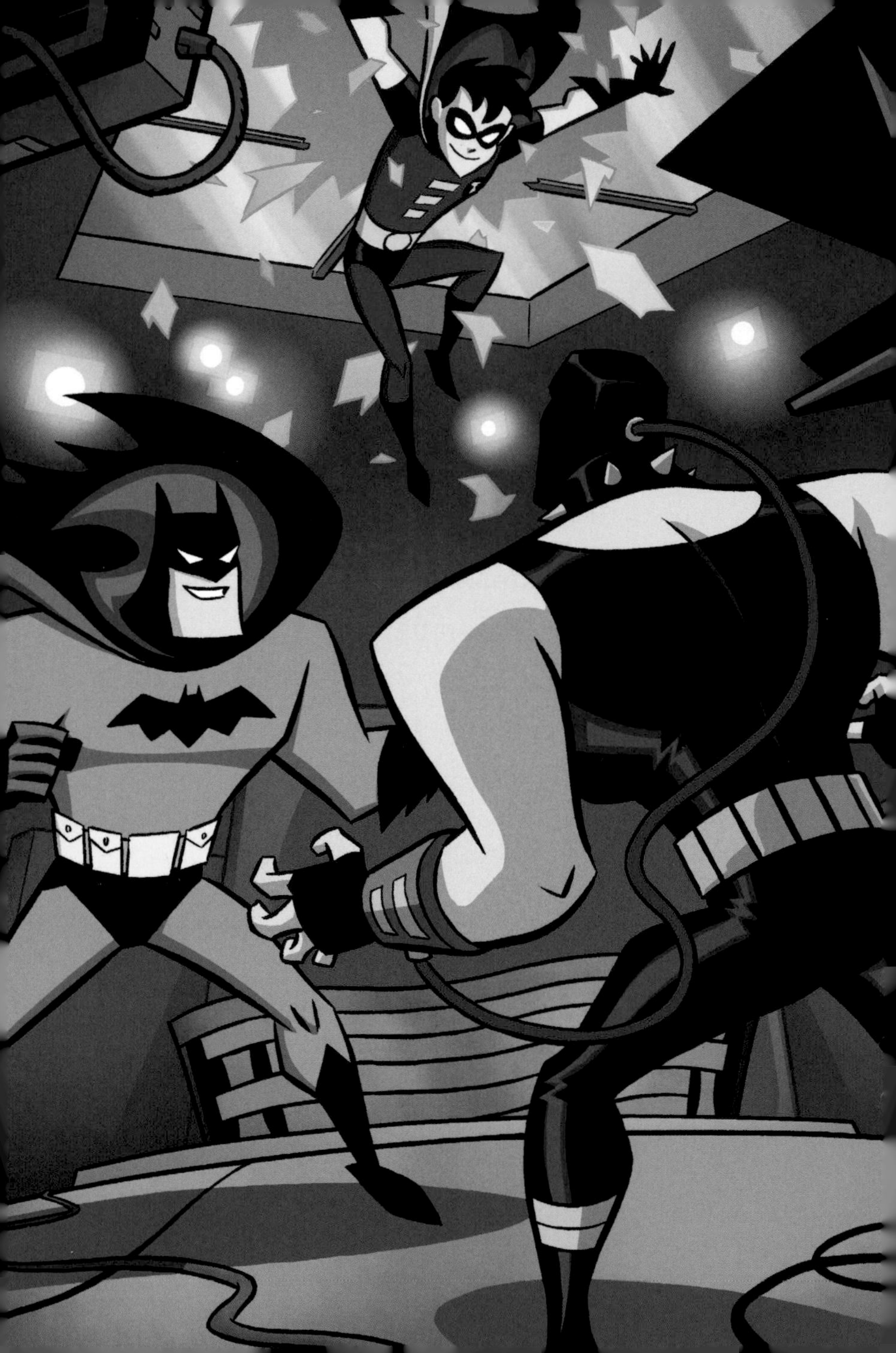

Bane turns on his heels and makes a run for the door. "This is only the beginning!" he shouts back at Batman and Robin.

As the Dynamic Duo race after Bane, the one thug still standing blocks the exit. He's holding Vicki in his grip.

"I gotta dispose of you," he growls. "Boss's orders. How about ladies first?"

As he leans in to hurt Vicki, she jams the heel of her shoe into his boot. Then she punches him in the face, and he crashes into a big TV camera.

"It's lights out for you, buster," Vicki snaps.

Batman is impressed. "Nice moves."

"Thank you," she says.

"Let's get Bane!" Robin cries.

Batman stops him. "Wait. Bane has something bigger planned, and it's happening right now."

Batman touches his earpiece. The small radio device inside his cowl picks up a broadcast from the police scanner.

Turn the page.

"There's a break-in at the First National Bank," Batman says. "Sounds like more of Bane's antics. Robin, you stay here and take care of business.

"You got it, Batman," replies the Boy Wonder. "I'll contact Commissioner Gordon and deliver these goons gift-wrapped."

Batman stands under the broken skylight and launches his grappling hook. "Can I hitch a ride?" Vicki asks.

"You're staying right here, Ms. Vale," Batman says. "Haven't you had enough excitement for one night?"

"Are you serious?" Vicki exclaims.

"I'm always serious," says Batman. Then he disappears into the night.

Turn to page 18.

Batman stays put to further assess the situation. He watches as the police sergeant calls out an order and one of the officers launches a canister of tear gas. It detonates in front of the thugs.

They cough and wheeze. Some rub their eyes and drop to their knees, while others make a run for it. Those are soon tackled by police officers.

All this excitement does not faze the muscle-bound bandit. He continues to stuff his satchels with piles of money. Then he turns and runs out of the bank, right into the cloud of tear gas!

The Caped Crusader continues to watch as the bank-robbing brute plows through the gas. The stinging spray has no effect on him. Police officers wearing gas masks advance on the perpetrator, but he rams right into them like an angry rhinoceros.

Then the muscleman leaps onto a police cruiser, denting the hood under his massive weight. *CRUNCH!*

Turn the page.

He uses this as a springboard and bounces straight into an open manhole. The thief has gone underground into the sewers.

Batman springs into action and goes after him, dropping down into a puddle of muddy water. *SPLASH!*

He follows the man's trail until he comes upon three tunnel entrances.

If he goes left, turn to page 63.
If he takes the middle one, turn to page 81.
If he goes right, turn to page 43.

Batman turns on his flashlight and enters the tunnel on the right. In the beam of light he sees the large man approach a metal grate. Using his bare hands, the bandit bends the iron bars in the grate until they are wide enough to fit his frame.

Once he is through, the bank robber bends the bars back into place.

*He's got super-strength*, Batman thinks to himself.

The Dark Knight produces a laser cutter from his Utility Belt and uses it on the iron grate. The red-hot beam slices through the metal, creating an opening for Batman.

The Caped Crusader passes through and continues his hunt.

Batman follows the man into an open space with concrete walls, but conceals himself in the shadows. There is a gurney in the center of the room, surrounded by scientific equipment. It is an underground laboratory.

Turn the page.

Lying on the gurney is another muscular man. A doctor stands over him. She is holding a vial filled with a glowing green liquid. Behind her, another large man enters. It is the villain Bane.

Bane was once an inmate who became the test subject of a government project to create superpowered soldiers and was pumped with a steroid called Venom. He became a chemically boosted brawler with enhanced endurance and super-strength.

Bane stole the Venom formula and escaped prison. Now it appeared he was creating more.

The bank robber crosses the room and hands the satchels of stolen money to Bane.

"Excellent work, Bruiser!" Bane says.

The thief pulls off his mask to reveal that he is the missing wrestler.

"Our first test subject is a success," Bane tells the doctor. "Here is your payment." He drops the money on the table between them. "Now start on the second!"

Bane points to the unconscious man on the gurney. Batman has a strong feeling that the second test subject is none other than Crusher, the other missing wrestler from Gotham Square Garden.

"Patience, Bane," replies the doctor. "These things must be done delicately."

"Indeed," Bane agrees. "I've selected only the strongest men in Gotham City on which to try out my latest batch of new and improved Venom. Once I have an army of superpowered soldiers under my command, the city will fall . . . along with its pathetic protector — Batman!"

The doctor is about to administer the Venom to the unconscious fighter.

Batman lunges from the shadows. Illuminated by the overhead lamp, the Caped Crusader cuts an imposing figure. Everyone in the room is momentarily stunned.

"Batman!" yells Bane. Then he turns to Bruiser. "You led him here!"

Turn the page.

"I'm canceling this appointment!" the Dark Knight growls.

"Initiate the procedure!" Bane screams at the doctor. Then he runs out of the room.

If Batman chases Bane to the surface, turn to page 47.

If Batman stops the doctor, turn to page 82.

Batman rushes out the door in pursuit of Bane.

"Yes, that's it, Batman," the villain taunts. "Follow me to your doom!"

They run down a dark corridor until they reach a set of metal double doors. Bane pushes through and climbs a ladder in the center of the room to a trapdoor in the ceiling. Once Batman enters, he stops to take in his surroundings.

The empty hallways lead to locker rooms and storage closets. Batman assumes they are now in a large gymnasium or athletic center. He follows Bane through the trapdoor and finds himself on a platform.

Batman discovers that he is standing in the center of the wrestling ring.

A bright spotlight shines down on Batman.

He turns to see that Bane's thugs are operating the audio and visual equipment. One of them is behind the large TV camera pointed at the ring.

Turn the page.

The jumbo screen overhead comes to life, showing a close-up of the fiendish felon's face.

"Good evening, Gotham City!" booms Bane in his best announcer's voice. "Let's get ready to rrrrrumble!!"

More lights turn on, and pulsing music blares through the loudspeakers. Bane enters the ring, cracking his knuckles and flexing his bulging biceps for the cameras.

"In case the World's Greatest Detective has yet to figure it out, this event is being televised live," Bane sneers. "That means all of your beloved city will see you lose . . . to me!"

Batman raises his fists and says, "Let the games begin."

Turn to page 50.

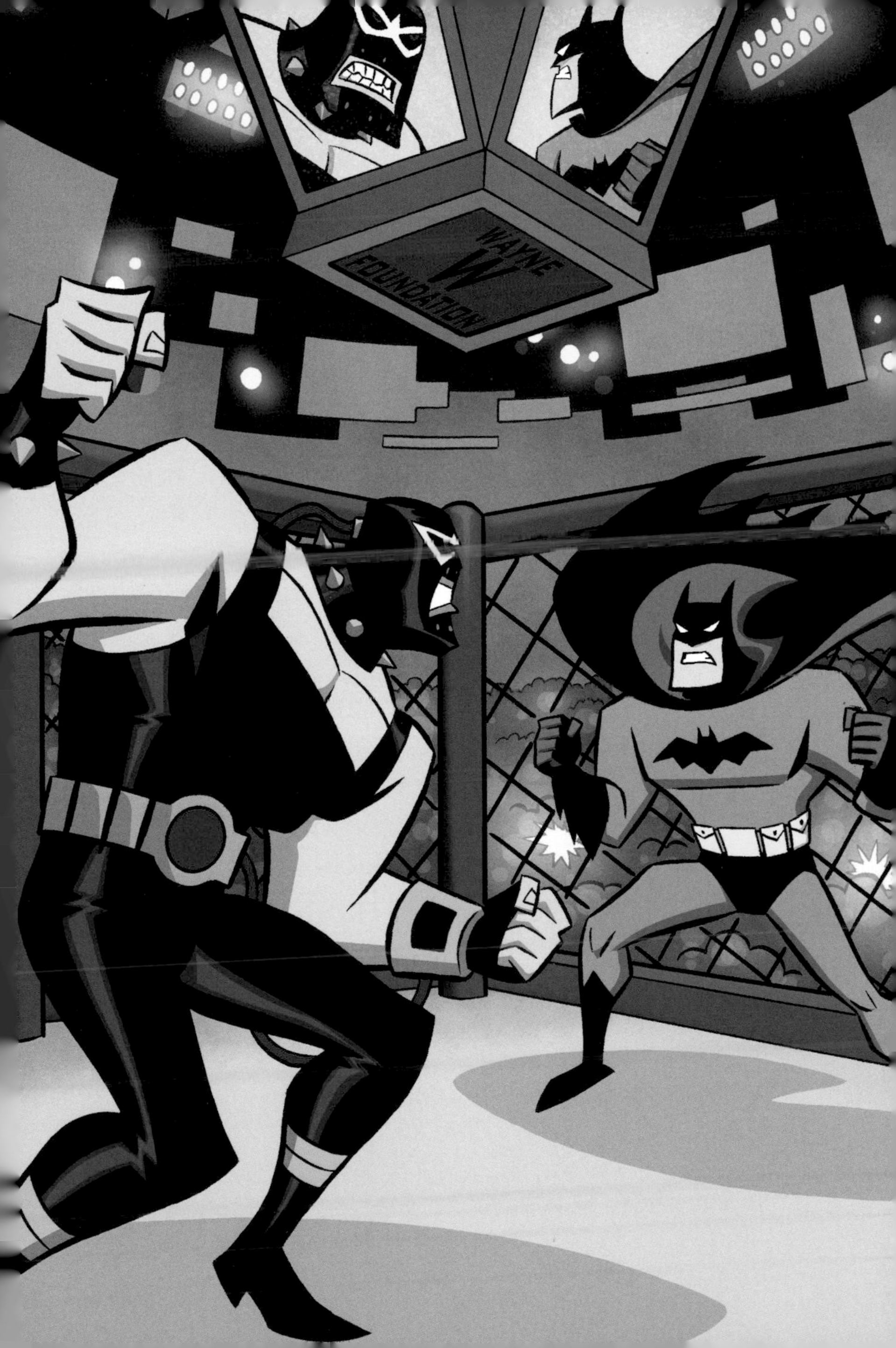
WAYNE
W
FOUNDATION

Bane leaps at Batman, performing a body drop. The Caped Crusader spins out of the way and delivers a back elbow maneuver that catches Bane between his shoulder blades. **CRACK!**

Stumbling forward, Bane uses the ropes to slingshot himself back at Batman.

The sheer force of Bane's trajectory knocks the Dark Knight off his feet, and the two foes tumble and roll across the mat. When they reach the edge, Bane comes out on top and pins Batman back.

"It appears you're down for the count!" he gloats. Bane raises his fists to pummel his opponent.

Batman wriggles free and reaches off the mat to grab a nearby folding chair. He swings the chair against Bane's chest. **CLANG!**

"Have a seat," Batman says.

Batman springs to his feet and faces off against his foe.

"Is that how you want to play?" Bane asks.

The villain activates his Venom dispenser. Glowing liquid pumps through the tube, and Bane grows in size.

Fueled by more than rage, Bane punches Batman clear across the ring. *POW!*

Luckily, the Dark Knight's armor sustains most of the impact. Bane's attack also gives Batman the distance he needs to make his next move. He produces several razor-sharp Batarangs from his belt. Batman hurls the Batarangs, and they slice through the villain's Venom tube.

The toxin sprays across the mat, causing the padded material to sizzle. Bane deflates as the chemical boost drains from his body.

"Blast you, Batman!" Bane bellows.

He charges at the hero with the intensity of a bull. Batman delivers the straight-armed clothesline maneuver that knocks Bane square onto his back.

"Your plan was a success," Batman says. "One of us *was* defeated and humiliated on live TV!"

Turn the page.

Then the super hero slaps the Bat-Cuffs on Bane.

Moments later, Commissioner Gordon and his squad enter the arena. They surround Bane and his thugs.

"By broadcasting your main event, you led my team straight to you," says the Commissioner. He orders his officers to round up the rogues and load them into the waiting police van.

"Bruiser and Crusher are down below and need medical attention," Batman states. "See that they get it!"

The Commissioner calls for an ambulance. Then he shakes the Dark Knight's hand. "Thank you, Batman. You've proven once again that *you* are the ultimate Gotham City Gladiator!"

**THE END**

To follow another path, turn to page 13.

Batman goes to Bruiser's residence. It is the penthouse of a high-rise luxury apartment building. The Caped Crusader climbs onto the balcony and finds the glass doors shattered and broken. Batman hears voices yelling within.

Upon entering, Batman discovers that the voices are really the television on at full volume. The entire apartment is in shambles; the couches are upturned, and the coffee table is splintered in half.

*These signs of foul play indicate more than one attacker,* Batman deduces. *The TV was just a ruse to drown out the sounds of a struggle.*

Suddenly, Batman senses footsteps behind him. He whirls around with a Batarang at the ready only to find a small gray cat peeking out from behind the couch. The friendly feline pads over to the Dark Knight and rubs her body against his boots. Looking down at his new furry friend, Batman notices a discolored spot on the hardwood floor — the first real clue in this investigation.

Turn the page.

Batman gets down on the floor to inspect the spot. Upon closer inspection, it is a drop of greenish-hued liquid. The area of the wood around it has been singed, showing that the drop might have acidic properties.

Reaching into his Utility Belt, Batman pulls out a small blade. He scrapes up the stained wood and places it into a small plastic bag. His plan is to take it back to the Batcave for a chemical analysis.

At that moment, the TV program is cut short by a breaking news brief.

"This is GNN correspondent Vicki Vale reporting live. I am en route to the First National Bank where, according to my sources, the Gotham City police force is up against a threat far more dangerous than the Joker!"

If Batman goes to the bank to help the police, turn to page 18.
If Batman goes to the Batcave to analyze the sample, turn to page 55.

Back at the Batcave, Batman analyzes the sample under a microscope. The ingredients in this compound all add up to something sinister: the same recipe that created one of Batman's most fearsome foes — Bane!

Bane was once an inmate at the Peña Duro prison. He became the test subject of a government project to create superpowered soldiers and was pumped with the steroid called Venom.

The test was a success, and Bane became a chemically boosted brawler with enhanced endurance and the strength to punch through solid brick! He stole the Venom formula and escaped the prison.

*Bane must be up to something big,* Batman thinks.

Suddenly, the Batcomputer relays that the alarm at the Second National Bank has been tripped. Batman is convinced this is not a coincidence and heads for the Batmobile.

Turn the page.

Roaring through the Batcave's hidden entrance, the Batmobile zooms into Gotham City. The sleek and silent vehicle pulls up to the bank while the robbery is in progress.

Several thugs have broken through the lobby's glass doors and are loading their bags with dollar bills. As soon as they turn toward the exit, they find it blocked by Batman.

The Caped Crusader recognizes the goons as Bane's men.

"Your transaction is unauthorized," he says.

Before the bank robbers can react, Batman pounces with lightning speed. *BAM! CRACK! WHACK!* After a brief struggle, Batman has rendered the thieves unconscious.

The police arrive to take them into custody, and Batman follows them to the station. Soon, the first thug to recover is brought into an interrogation room.

If Batman interrogates the robber himself, turn to page 57.
If Batman lets the police interrogate the robber, turn to page 94.

Batman enters the interrogation room, and the criminal scoffs.

"Well, if it isn't the bogeyman," he snorts.

Batman ignores the snide remark and asks, "Where's Bane? What's his plan?"

"I don't know," the thug says. "Besides, you can't do anything to me. I know my rights."

"Rights? That's where you're wrong!" growls the Dark Knight.

He locks the door so the police cannot enter and grabs the thug by the collar. Batman lifts the criminal into the air. "Got anything to say now?" he asks.

"I will not ask again," Batman says.

The scared bank robber squeals and divulges the location of Bane's secret lair.

"It's in the sewers! When you get to the three tunnels, take the one on the right."

"Why were you robbing the bank?" Batman asks.

Turn the page.

"He . . . he . . . needs the cash to fund some expensive project. He's buying chemicals for some sort of potion. That's all I know, I swear!"

Batman releases him. The thug drops to his knees and kisses the dirty floor.

The Dark Knight unlocks the door and heads for the sewers. There isn't a moment to lose!

Batman opens a manhole and descends into the maze-like sewer system beneath Gotham City. After several twists and turns, the Dark Knight finally reaches the tunnel that the thug described.

The path is blocked by an iron grate. Batman produces a miniature laser cutter from his Utility Belt and slices through the metal bars.

Moments later, Batman makes his way to an open space with concrete walls. Remaining hidden in the shadows, the detective observes two gurneys in the center of the room, surrounded by scientific equipment. It is an underground laboratory.

Lying on the gurneys are two muscular men. Batman recognizes them as the missing wrestlers, Bruiser and Crusher. A doctor is standing between them. She is holding a vial filled with a glowing green liquid. Behind her, another large man enters. It is Batman's archenemy, Bane.

"Excellent work, doctor!" Bane says.

"Our first test subject is a success," she tells him. "Bruiser's biology has responded well to the serum."

"Indeed," Bane agrees. "I've selected only the strongest men in Gotham to try out my latest batch of new and improved Venom. Once I have an entire army under my command, the city will belong to me!"

The doctor is about to administer the Venom to the unconscious fighter.

The Dark Knight emerges from the shadows. The villains are momentarily stunned.

"Batman!" yells Bane.

Turn the page.

"I'm canceling this appointment!" the hero growls.

"Initiate the procedure!" Bane screams at the doctor. Then he shoves past Batman and disappears down the tunnel.

If Batman chases Bane through the sewers, turn to page 61.
If Batman stops the doctor, turn to page 102.

Batman chases Bane down the winding sewer paths. The hero is hot on the villain's heels. Bane comes upon a large overflow outlet that leads out into the East River. His boots slip across some slime, and he falls flat on his back.

Batman jumps on Bane, pinning him down. The two men wrestle in the raw sewage.

"You certainly fight dirty, Batman!" Bane grunts. "Then again, so do I!"

The muscular menace presses a button in his glove, activating the Venom dispenser. Glowing green liquid pumps through the pipe attached to the back of Bane's mask and directly into the brawler's head. His biceps bulge, and his entire mass increases before Batman's eyes.

"After I break you, all will know that BANE is the ultimate Gotham City Gladiator!"

Bane roars with rage and pushes Batman.

The Caped Crusader stumbles backward. "I won't let you drag my name through the mud," he says.

Turn the page.

Reaching into his Utility Belt, Batman finds a mini flash bomb. As Bane charges toward him, the hero shields his eyes and detonates the device.

### FLASH!

"ARRGH!" Bane screams. "I can't see!"

"Then you won't know what hit you!" Batman replies. He punches Bane square in the jaw. **POW!**

The attack has little effect on the chemically boosted brute. Batman unleashes a flurry of punches and kicks against his opponent. Each hit brings him a step closer to the edge of the tunnel.

Seconds later, Bane loses his footing and falls toward the river.

With lightning-fast reflexes, Batman hurls the Batrope at Bane and snares his arm. The Dark Knight pulls his enemy back onto the ledge.

"You've lost, Bane," Batman says. "I'm bringing you to Arkham Asylum where you can be rehabilitated."

"Bah! No cage can hold *this* beast," Bane yells.

He pulls the Batrope into his mouth and bites it with his teeth. ***CHOMP!***

"Until next time, Batman!" he cries. The rope snaps, and Bane plummets into the churning water below.

***SPLASH!***

Batman waits for several minutes, but Bane's body never surfaces. He knows in his gut that they will cross paths again. This is not the end of Bane.

Batman turns back to save the wrestlers and put an end to Bane's evil plot.

**THE END**

To follow another path, turn to page 13.

Batman takes the left tunnel and turns on his flashlight. After a few minutes, he reaches a metal staircase that leads up to a padlocked door. The Dark Knight deftly picks the lock and enters. He is in a basement or storage area. Judging from the number of folding chairs and equipment piled within, it must be an athletic center or sports venue. At the far end is a ladder that leads through a door in the ceiling. Batman climbs up and enters another dark room.

Before he can click on his night-vision goggles to investigate, a spotlight blinds him. He turns away and takes in his surroundings. The rest of the lights come on, and the Dark Knight discovers he is standing in the center of the large ring in Gotham Square Garden.

"Thank you for graciously accepting my challenge!" booms a voice from above. Batman knows immediately that it belongs to Bane.

"Before we battle, my boys here will soften you up so that I may break you!" yells the villain.

Right on cue, several of Bane's men enter the arena. They are carrying clubs and chains and other weapons.

"And now for my little surprise," Bane continues. "Meet the newest recruits in my army!"

Batman sees the hulking shapes of two muscular men. When they step into the light, Batman recognizes them instantly — Bruiser and Crusher. Their muscles bulge and their veins pop. The missing wrestlers are now pumped full of Bane's super-serum Venom . . . and they are itching for a fight!

If Batman takes on Bane's men by himself, turn to page 95.
If Batman calls for backup, turn to page 67.

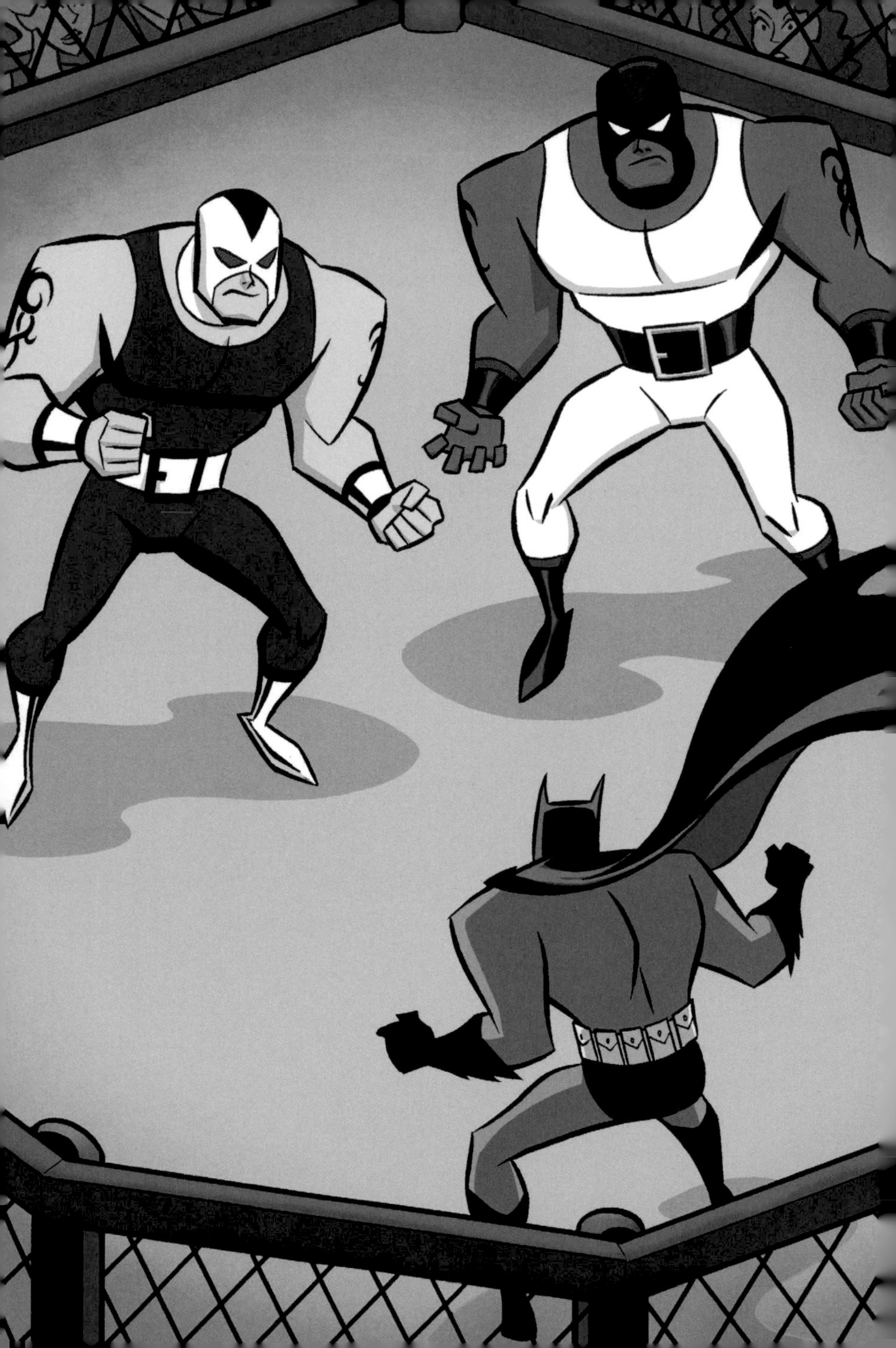

Batman taps a button on his Utility Belt, sending out a mysterious signal. Then he throws a handful of gas pellets at the advancing brawlers.

***POOM! POOM! POOM!*** The cloud of smoke causes the thugs to cough and wheeze.

Batman shoots his grapnel gun up at the rafters and soars away from the henchmen. Bane sees this and leaps into action. He bounds across the beams to where Batman is ascending.

"What's your hurry?" Bane asks. "The fun has just begun!"

The villain grabs the Batrope and bites through it with his teeth. ***CHOMP!***

Batman loses his grip and plummets into the sea of fighters below. They tear and pull at the Dark Knight's cape as he struggles to break free.

"You are no match for my army!" Bane bellows.

"That's why I called my own," Batman responds.

Turn the page.

At that moment, the double doors on either side of the arena burst open. ***CLANG! BANG!***

Three masked figures rush into the room. They are Batman's crime-fighting partners — Robin, Batgirl, and Nightwing!

The acrobatic heroes swing over the ropes and land inside the ring. They rush to Batman's side.

"You rang, Big Guy?" says Robin with a smile.

"Looks like we evened the odds," adds Batgirl.

"It's a triple threat!" exclaims Nightwing.

Bane scoffs and addresses his men. "Bah, these masked mice are no match for us. Exterminate them!"

"We'll see about that," Batman says. Then he doles out his battle strategy. "Robin and Batgirl, you're on containment duty. Nightwing, you follow my lead!"

Batman barrels through the thugs with Nightwing close behind. Together, the daring duo tackles Bruiser and Crusher to the ground.

Robin and Batgirl cartwheel to opposite sides of the ring and begin picking off the thugs as if it were just another target practice in the Batcave. Unleashing a barrage of Batarangs, smoke capsules, and mini flash bombs, the thugs soon fall to their knees under the relentless attack.

Then the junior heroes jump into the fray. Using swift kicks and karate chops, Robin and Batgirl relieve the goons of their weapons and then of their senses.

### BAM! WHAP! CRACK!

Meanwhile, Batman and Nightwing face off against the fighters. With their renewed strength and speed, Bruiser and Crusher break free from the heroes and hurl them onto the mat. Then the brawlers charge at Batman and Nightwing like a couple of rampaging rhinos!

Luckily, Batman and Nightwing are expertly trained in many forms of combat — including wrestling. They each sidestep the oncoming attack and parry with two back kicks.

### WHAP! WHAP!

Turn to page 71.

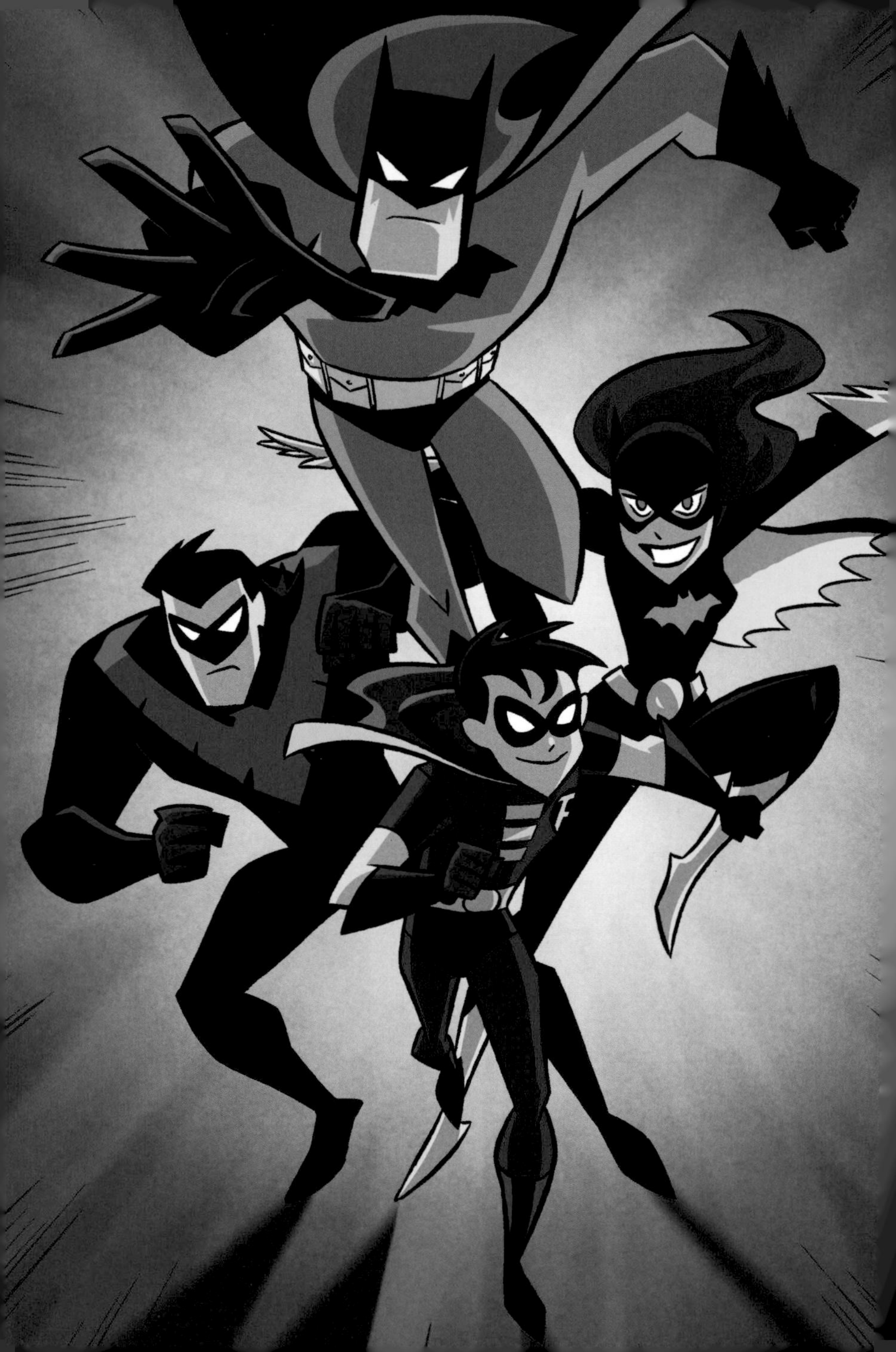

Bruiser and Crusher stumble headfirst into the ropes and rebound toward the Dynamic Duo. Batman performs an elbow drop. **POW!** Nightwing delivers a double forearm smash. **KA·POW!** The chemically boosted brawlers are momentarily stunned.

"Here!" Batman cries and lobs a small vial to Nightwing. "It is an antidote that will counter the effects of the Venom."

When Bruiser and Crusher rush at Batman and Nightwing, the two heroes somersault over the brutes, causing them to head-butt each other. **SMASH!**

With the fighters dazed, Batman and Nightwing administer the antidote. The fighters shrink back to their normal size in mere seconds!

"Whoa," Bruiser says, rubbing his head. "I feel a little woozy."

"What happened?" Crusher asks.

"You almost had a double knockout," Nightwing replies.

Turn the page.

Batman catches Bane rushing for the exit out of the corner of his eye. "Not so fast," he says and shoots his grappling hook at the rafters above.

### WHOOSH!

Bane cackles as he nears the double doors. He is inches away from escaping when a black shadow blocks his path.

"BATMAN!" Bane yells.

"We have unfinished business," Batman says.

Bane steps back and bumps into Nightwing. Then he turns left and right only to find Batgirl and Robin flanking him.

"It's your move," says Batgirl.

"Bah, I will chew all of you up and spit out your bones!" Bane bellows.

Just then, Commissioner Gordon and a team of officers burst into the arena.

"Freeze and put your hands up!" commands the Commissioner.

Robin looks around and laughs. "I hope you're really hungry, Bane!"

Bane grudgingly raises his arms. Soon, he and his men are carted off to jail.

Batman proves once again he is Gotham City's ultimate protector . . . even with a little help from him friends!

**THE END**

To follow another path, turn to page 13.

Batman crashes into the studio. His entrance startles the criminals.

"Batman! You are ahead of schedule," says Bane. "You must be *eager* to lose."

"Give up, Bane!" Batman growls.

"Oh, no. This is not the grand arena I had in mind," Bane replies. "Besides, I want you to see my special surprise."

Batman advances and the thugs close in around him.

"Take another step and those missing men will die!" Bane threatens. "You must wait until our battle in front of the cameras," he continues. "Then Gotham City will know that *I* am the real warrior. Those men are part of my ultimate plan!"

Batman considers if the lives of Bruiser and Crusher are in danger, or if Bane is bluffing.

If Batman lets Bane go, turn to page 75.
If Batman ignores the threat and attacks, turn to page 99.

Batman agrees to let Bane go, but obviously does not trust the scheming scoundrel. As Bane and his men turn to leave, Batman shoots a tiny tracking device onto Bane's back.

Once they are gone, Batman climbs back up to the roof with his grappling hook and enters the Batplane. He immediately logs into his mobile Batcomputer and the radar picks up the tracking signal.

"Gotcha!" Batman says.

He follows the signal to the edge of town near the river. Bane's hideout is located underground in the maze of tunnels and passageways that make up Gotham City's sewer system.

Batman dives into a manhole and continues his search for Bane.

Batman follows the signal through the twisting, turning sewers and into an open space with concrete walls. There is an empty gurney in the center of the room, surrounded by scientific equipment. It is an underground science lab.

Turn the page.

Bane enters with two large, muscular men on either side of him. Batman recognizes them as Bruiser and Crusher. Only they look different — bigger, meaner, and stronger.

"We keep running into each other," Bane sneers. "Now you know my secret. I've selected only the strongest men in Gotham City to try out my latest batch of new and improved Venom. Once I have an army of superpowered soldiers under my command, the city will fall . . . along with its pathetic protector — you!"

"Have you gone mad?" Batman growls. "Using these innocent men as guinea pigs in your twisted scheme!"

"Guilty as charged," replies Bane. "These two test subjects are a perfect success. Let me show you."

Bane turns to the chemically boosted brawlers and says, "We have a rodent infesting our lair. Exterminate him!"

"Yes, sir!" Bruiser and Crusher say together.

They charge at Batman, but the hero's reflexes are lightning fast. He pushes the gurney into their path and they tumble over it. *CRASH!*

Then Batman jumps up and grabs onto the overhead lamp. When the fighters get up, he swings across the room and knocks them back down with his boots. *BAM!*

Suddenly, the Venom within Bruiser and Crusher kicks into high gear.

Bruiser's biceps begin to bulge. Crusher clenches his fists and jaw. Their bodies seem to be growing in mass.

Together, they grab Batman and pull him down to the ground. The Caped Crusader struggles in their vice-like grip.

"Are you enjoying my master plan in action, Batman?" Bane asks with a laugh. "Hmm. I've always wondered what it would be like to see Gotham City's greatest guardian under the influence of my patented serum. Let's find out, shall we?"

Turn the page.

Batman grunts against his captors, but it is no use. They are too strong, even for him.

"If you can't beat 'em, join 'em!" says Crusher.

Bane prepares to pump Batman full of Venom. Nobody knows what effect the toxin will have on the Dark Knight, but Gotham City is in for a shocking surprise!

**THE END**

To follow another path, turn to page 13.

Bruiser barrels toward Batman, but the Dark Knight is ready. He pulls a small canister from his belt and aims it at Bruiser's face — releasing a spray of sleeping gas! *FSSSSSSSST!*

Bruiser stops in his tracks. He coughs and wheezes and rubs his eyes, but the gas has no effect on him other than to infuriate him more.

"ARRRRGH!" Bruiser roars.

*He's still standing!* Batman says to himself. *This is going to be harder than I thought.*

Batman produces a taser and zaps the raging wrestler. *ZZZZARK!*

The high voltage of electricity shocks Bruiser, and he falls face-first onto the floor.

"The bigger they are, the harder they fall," Batman says.

"He sure is out for the count," adds the Commissioner. "Thank you, Batman."

With the help of three police officers, Batman carries Bruiser's bulky, unconscious body to a waiting ambulance.

Turn the page.

While the emergency medical technicians tend to Bruiser, Batman stealthily procures a blood sample from the fighter for his own analysis in the Batcave.

"Hopefully we will get to the bottom of this mystery soon," the Commissioner says to Batman.

When the policeman turns to face the Dark Knight, the hero is already gone.

Turn to page 55.

Batman enters the middle tunnel. He turns on his flashlight and follows the path until it veers to the right. Moments later, the Caped Crusader hears the soft pitter-patter of footsteps behind him.

Batman grips his Batarang and whirls around. The flashlight's beam shows — absolutely nothing.

Suddenly, something skitters across Batman's boots. He shines the light down and sees a giant sewer rat! *SCREE! SCREE! SCREE!*

The Dark Knight shakes his head and continues on his way. For what seems like minutes, Batman finally reaches the end of the tunnel . . . only to find a concrete wall. This path was a dead end, and so Batman heads back to try one of the other entrances.

**THE END**

To follow another path, turn to page 13.

Quick as a flash, Batman hurls a Batarang at the doctor's wrist, knocking the serum from her hand. The vial falls to the ground and shatters.

As the glowing liquid oozes out across the floor, it begins to sizzle and burn. **FSSSS!**

"Look what you've done!" she screams. "Do you know how long it took to make that batch?"

"Probably not as long as you'll be spending in jail," Batman replies.

The doctor rubs her wrist and yells, "Batman has breached the bunker!"

In an instant, more of Bane's thugs come rushing in. Batman sizes them up and prepares to strike — when suddenly — he is blindsided by Bruiser. **BAM!**

The titanic wrestler tackles Batman to the ground with a body slam. Then he picks up the Dark Knight and holds him high overhead.

Reaching into his Utility Belt, Batman slides out a miniature flash bomb and detonates it in Bruiser's face. **CHOOM!**

"ARGH! MY EYES!" Bruiser cries and drops the Dark Knight.

Batman nimbly lands on his feet. As Bruiser charges blindly at the hero, Batman uses the brute's momentum to spin him into the oncoming horde of thugs like a human battering ram. **SLAM!**

The goons drop as if they were bowling pins, piling up in front of the door. The doctor scrambles to climb over the fallen men and escape.

Batman hurls a bolo with precision at the fleeing foe. The coils rapidly wrap around the doctor, ensnaring her. She, too, falls onto the pile before the door.

"Sit tight," Batman says.

The hero hurries over to Bruiser and administers an all-purpose antidote that he keeps in his Utility Belt.

Within seconds, Bruiser's body shrinks and his pupils focus on the Caped Crusader.

Turn the page.

"Batman!" he exclaims, looking around. "Where am I? What happened?"

The Dark Knight briefly explains the situation as he unties Crusher from the gurney. Batman finds some smelling salts on a nearby tray and uses them to revive the wrestler.

Crusher wakes up woozy and disoriented. "Did I win?" he asks.

"Only in your dreams," Bruiser answers. "Bane turned us into lab rats along with the real rats down here in the sewer."

"Say what?" Crusher cries. "Let me at him!"

"He's gone," Batman states. "I've contacted the police to pick up his criminal cohorts and bring you medical assistance. As soon as I find Bane, we'll be having a rematch!"

"When you do, give us a call," Crusher says. "We'll tag-team him with you!"

"Speaking of which, you still owe me a fight. Or are you too chicken?" Bruiser says to Crusher. Then he starts flapping his arms and clucking.

"Don't embarrass yourself, man," Crusher replies. "Go home while you're still standing."

"Hey, Batman!" Bruiser calls out. "Which one of us would win in a fight?"

But when the brawlers turn around, they find that the Dark Knight has disappeared.

**THE END**

To follow another path, turn to page 13.

Batman strikes with lightning speed. He removes two tiny razor-sharp Batarangs from his Utility Belt and hurls them at Bane. The pointy projectiles nick Bane's arm and then embed themselves into the wall behind him.

**THUNK! THUNK!**

Bane releases his grip on Vicki. The scared journalist sprints across the room and hides behind the news anchor desk.

"Cute trick," Bane says, removing the Batarangs and then snapping them with his bare hands. **SNAP! SNAP!**

"I've got one, too. Care to see it?" Bane activates the Venom pump with his fist, and the chemical begins to flow through the pipe on his arm and into his head.

Vicki stares in horror as Bane increases in size. His upper body ripples and bulges and strains against his shirt. To display his newfound power, Bane saunters over to the large news camera and tears the metal device in half. **SKEERUNCH!!**

"See what I did there?" Bane asks. "And I will do the same to you, Batman. All without breaking a sweat."

The news camera gives Vicki an idea. She pulls out her phone and starts recording the events taking place.

Batman sees her out of the corner of his eye and turns to Bane. "You wanted your fifteen minutes of fame, Bane," the hero says. "Enjoy them while they last, because your time is up!"

Bane lifts the mangled, twisted metal that was once the news camera and throws it at Batman. "Catch!" he cries.

The Caped Crusader backflips safely out of the way of the flying wreckage.

Bane crosses the room toward the news desk and pounds it with both fists. **SMASH!** The structure cracks and crumbles.

Vicki screams and runs from her hiding place. The bulging brawler lifts up a chunk of desk and throws it toward the reporter.

Turn the page.

In the blink of an eye, Batman shoots his grappling hook, looping it around Vicki's waist. Then he pulls her out of harm's way a split second before the desk crashes.

"Thank you, Batman," Vicki says nervously. "Talk about late breaking news!"

"Enough games!" Batman growls. "Tell me what you did with the wrestlers."

"No more talking!" shouts Bane. "More fighting!"

The muscular man cracks his knuckles and charges like a rhino toward Batman and Vicki.

Thinking quickly, the Dark Knight pushes Vicki to the ground and drops down alongside her. Bane continues his trajectory and crashes right through the studio wall! *BAM!*

Turn to page 90.

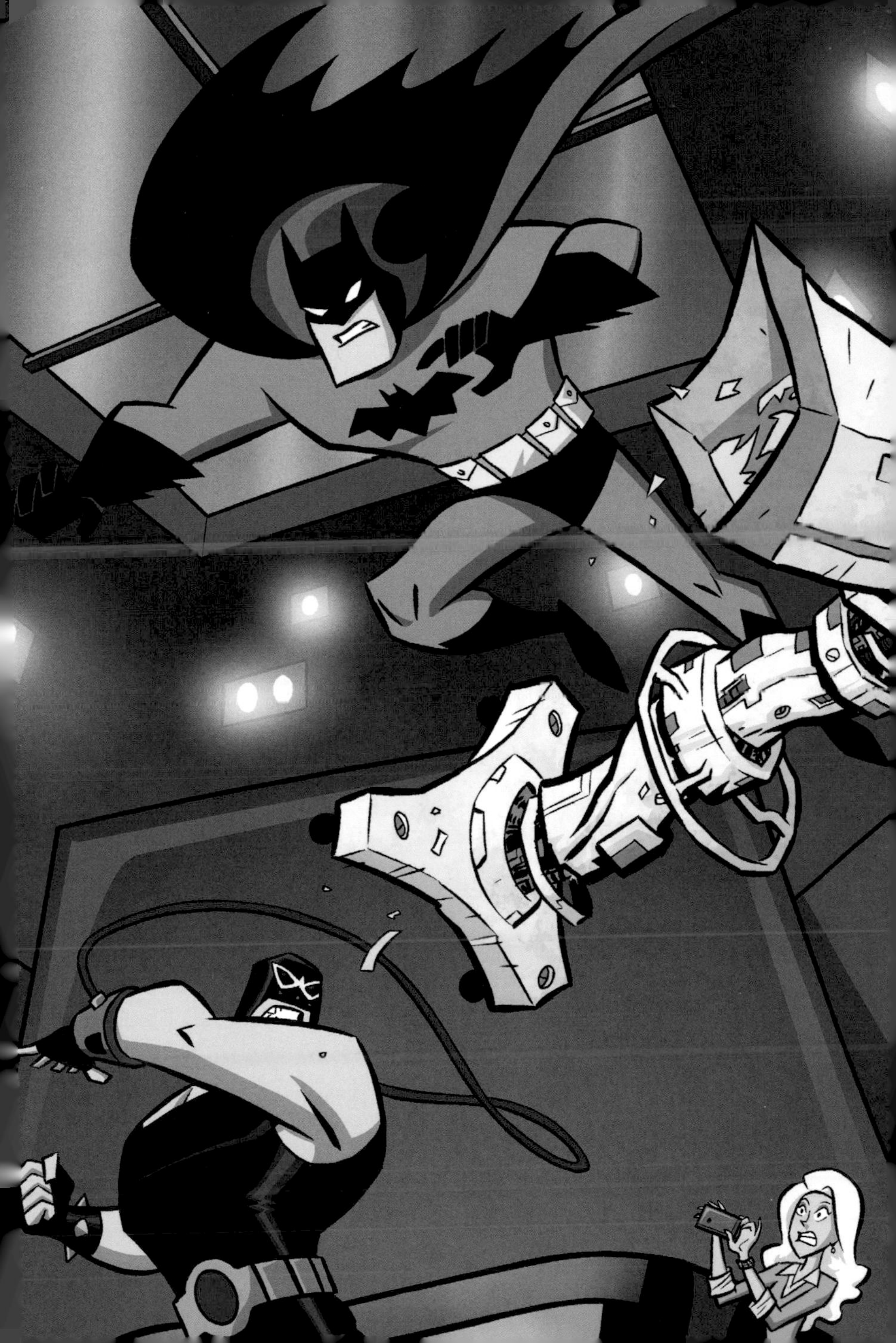

Batman pulls his cape over himself and Vicki to protect them from the falling debris. Meanwhile, Bane plummets to the ground below. He lands in a big metal Dumpster and is knocked out cold. ***CLANG!***

Together, Batman and Vicki peer out of the giant hole in the studio wall. They see Bane's hulking form buried among the trash.

"Well, he did like to make an entrance . . . and an exit," Vicki quips. "Now what?"

"I call the Commissioner and we cart Bane off to a nice padded cell at Arkham Asylum," Batman replies. "After his beauty sleep, we'll question him about the missing wrestlers and hopefully put this case to rest."

**THE END**

To follow another path, turn to page 13.

On the rooftop of police headquarters, Commissioner Gordon waits next to the Bat-Signal. He senses a slight flutter behind him and turns around. Batman is perched on the ledge like a gargoyle.

The Commissioner gasps and says, "I'll never get used to that."

"Bane is back," Batman says. He tells the policeman what happened at the arena.

"Interesting," Commissioner Gordon replies. "Bruiser's manager called, saying Bruiser never showed up at the Garden. He's not answering his phone, and he's not at his apartment."

"I believe both of these events are connected," Batman says. "There is no such thing as a coincidence. Not in Gotham City, anyway."

Turn to page 93.

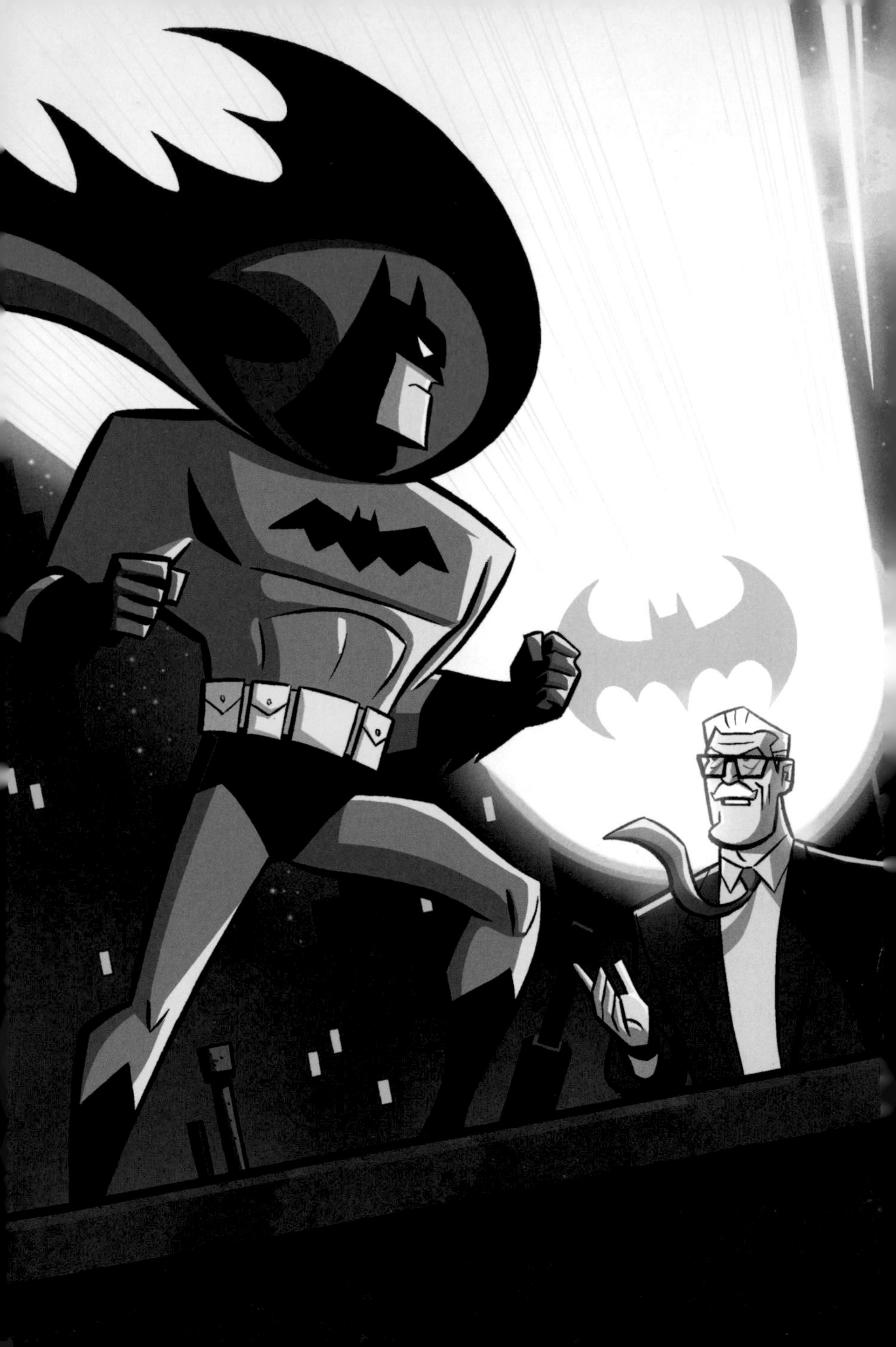

The Commissioner hands Batman a small slip of paper. "That's Bruiser's address," he says. "You have the reputation of being the World's Greatest Detective. See if you can find any clues that will help us solve this mystery."

Suddenly, the roof door bursts open. A young policeman runs toward the Commissioner.

"Sir, we have a situation," he pants.

"What is it, Officer Henry?" asks Gordon.

"There has been a break-in at the First National Bank. The officers on call say it's nothing they've ever dealt with before!"

"I doubt this is a coincidence," Batman says.

The voice startles Officer Henry. "Is that who I think it is?" he asks.

As his eyes adjust, they make out a pointy-eared silhouette against the full moon. In a split second, it's gone.

"No comment," replies Commissioner Gordon.

If Batman goes to the bank to help the police, turn to page 18.
If he goes to Bruiser's apartment to search for clues, turn to page 53.

Batman melds into the shadows as the police commence their interrogation of the thug.

"I know my rights," cries the crony. "I ain't saying nothin' until my lawyer shows up."

Smirking at the detectives, the thug puts his feet on the desk and folds his arms behind his head.

Batman paces behind the two-way mirror.

"We're losing precious time," he says to Commissioner Gordon.

"We are required by law to call his lawyer," the Commissioner reminds Batman.

The Dark Knight grunts. As Commissioner Gordon goes to use the telephone, Batman makes his move.

Turn to page 57.

Batman sizes up his opponents and quickly devises a clever strategy. As the musclemen advance, the Caped Crusader reaches into his Utility Belt and produces a small but powerful EMP device. This gadget emits an electro-magnetic pulse that can sap the energy from any machine powered by electricity.

Bruiser and Crusher are now standing on opposite sides of Batman.

"It's lights out for the Dark Knight!" Crusher cries.

Bruiser and Bane's thugs howl with laughter.

"My thoughts exactly," Batman replies and activates the EMP device. **ZAP!**

The overhead lights spark and sputter and turn off, plunging the arena into darkness.

Batman clicks on his night-vision goggles. Everything around him is outlined in an eerie glow. He can see clearly while the other men fumble around with confusion.

Turn the page.

Batman puts his second plan into action. He shoves Bruiser with all of his might. Then he ducks. Bruiser turns and takes a swing, punching Crusher right in the jaw. *KA-POW!*

"I got 'im!" Bruiser cries. "I got Bat —" *POW!*

Crusher swings back and punches Bruiser in the gut.

"No, *I* got 'im!" shouts Crusher.

Bruiser gets behind Crusher and puts him in a headlock. Crusher breaks free and flips Bruiser onto the mat. *THUD!*

The Caped Crusader steps back as the beefy brawlers battle each other.

While Bruiser and Crusher continue to duke it out, Batman turns his attention to Bane's henchmen. He throws Batarangs at them, knocking the weapons from their hands.

This allows Batman to get in close proximity and disable each thug with several martial arts techniques. Some are tougher to take down than others, but Batman is very thorough.

Suddenly, the overhead generator lights kick in, illuminating the arena.

The action stops. Crusher looks down at the man he's pinned to the mat and realizes that it's not Batman — but Bruiser! The real Caped Crusader is to their left, surrounded by a pile of Bane's unconscious thugs.

"Impressive," Bane yells. "You truly are a *dark knight*." Then he leaps from the rafters and lands on the mat near Batman. "Prepare for the final round!"

Before Batman can react, Bruiser and Crusher ambush him from behind. They overpower the Caped Crusader by grabbing his arms and pinning them behind his back.

"Good work," Bane tells the brawlers. Then he turns to Batman. "In case you get any ideas, let's relieve you of this troublesome tool belt."

The villain removes Batman's Utility Belt.

"HA! You're not so tough without your toys, are ya?" taunts Bruiser.

Turn the page.

"Careful," adds Crusher. "He may be hiding something else!"

"Indeed," says Bane rubbing his chin. "Let's see how powerful the Dark Knight is when his most effective weapon is taken away!"

Then Bane pulls off Batman's mask.

**THE END**

To follow another path, turn to page 13.

Batman moves to attack Bane, and the thugs close in around him.

"You'll have to get through us," one of them says.

"I could use a warm-up," Batman replies.

The Caped Crusader grabs the nearest thug and performs a judo throw, hurling the goon over his shoulder. The man crashes onto the desk.

More thugs lunge at Batman. In rapid succession, the Dark Knight delivers an uppercut punch, a roundhouse kick, and then a ground sweep. *WHAP! CRACK! SMACK!*

Watching Batman in action is a wonder to behold. His movements are precise and fluid. In seconds, Bane's henchmen are left groaning and gagging and nursing their wounds.

Bane is furious and hollers at his henchmen. "Clearly you're all overpaid! He is just one man!"

"Not just any man," the hero says with a smirk. "I'm Batman."

Turn the page.

He takes a step closer to Bane. Bane takes a step closer to Batman. The foes stare each other down.

Suddenly, the silence is pierced by a woman's scream.

"AIEEEEEEEE!"

"Hey boss, lookee here!" shouts a thug entering the room. "I found her snooping around outside."

He walks in with someone struggling in his grip. It is Vicki Vale.

"Ah, Ms. Vale, I have your top story right here," Bane says. "Let's see if you live long enough to tell it!"

Bane grabs Vicki and holds her wrist in his vice-like grip.

"Unhand me, you creep!" she yells and kicks at Bane's shins, but the villain only laughs.

"I like this one," Bane says to Batman. "She shows more guts than these pitiful clowns in my employ."

"Let her go, Bane," Batman orders.

The villain smiles cruelly and tightens his grip on Vicki. She grimaces.

"I need only apply the slightest pressure, Batman," Bane says. "You know what I want. Just leave me be so that I may carry on with my plans."

Batman tenses. The seconds tick slowly, and the Caped Crusader makes a decision.

Turn to page 86.

Quick as a flash, Batman hurls a Batarang at the doctor's wrist, knocking the serum from her hand. The vial falls to the ground and shatters. ***SKEESH!***

As the glowing liquid oozes out across the floor, it begins to sizzle and burn.

***FSSSS!***

"Look what you've done!" she screams. "Do you know how long it took to make that batch?"

"Probably not as long as you'll be spending in jail," Batman replies.

The doctor rubs her wrist and yells into a nearby intercom. "Batman has breached the bunker!"

In an instant, more of Bane's thugs come rushing in. Batman sizes them up and prepares to strike—when suddenly—he is blindsided by Bruiser. ***BAM!***

The titanic wrestler tackles Batman to the ground with a body slam. Then he picks up the Dark Knight and holds him high overhead.

Reaching into his Utility Belt, Batman slides out a miniature flash bomb and detonates it.

**CHOOM!**

"ARGH! MY EYES!" Bruiser cries, dropping the Dark Knight.

Batman nimbly lands on his feet. As Bruiser charges blindly at the hero, Batman uses the brute's momentum to spin him into the oncoming horde of thugs like a human battering ram. **SLAM!**

The goons drop as if they were bowling pins, piling up in front of the door. The doctor scrambles to climb over the men and escape.

Batman hurls a bolo with expert accuracy at the fleeing foe. The coils rapidly wrap around the doctor, ensnaring her. She, too, falls onto the pile before the door.

"Sit tight," Batman says.

The hero hurries over to Bruiser and administers an all-purpose antidote that he keeps in his Utility Belt.

Turn the page.

Within seconds, Bruiser's body shrinks back to normal and his pupils focus on the Caped Crusader.

"Batman!" he exclaims, looking around. "Where am I? What happened?"

The Dark Knight briefly explains the situation as he unties Crusher from the gurney. Batman gets some smelling salts from the doctor's tray and uses them to revive the wrestler.

Crusher wakes up woozy and disoriented. "Did I win?" he asks.

"Only in your dreams," Bruiser answers. "Bane turned us into his lab rats along with the real rats down here in the sewer."

"Say what?" Crusher cries. "Let me at him!"

"He's gone," Batman states. "I've contacted the police to pick up his criminal cohorts and bring you medical assistance. As soon as I find Bane, we'll be having a rematch!"

"When you do, give us a call," Crusher says. "We'll tag-team him with you!"

"Speaking of which, you still owe me a fight. Or are you too chicken?" Bruiser says to Crusher. Then he starts flapping his arms and clucking.

"Don't embarrass yourself, man," Crusher replies. "Go home while you can still eat solid food."

"Hey, Batman!" Bruiser calls out. "Which one of us do you think would win in a fight?"

The brawlers turn around and find that the Dark Knight has disappeared.

**THE END**

To follow another path, turn to page 13.

# AUTHOR

*New York Times* bestselling author John Sazaklis enjoys writing children's books about his favorite characters. He has also illustrated Spider-Man books and created toys used in *MAD* magazine. To him, it's a dream come true! John lives with his beautiful wife in New York City.

# ILLUSTRATOR

Ethen Beavers is a professional comic book artist from Modesto, California. His best-known works for DC Comics include Justice League Unlimited and Legion of Super-Heroes in the 31st Century. He has also illustrated for other top publishers, including Marvel, Dark Horse, and Abrams.

# GLOSSARY

**archenemy** (arch-EN-uh-mee)—one's main or principle foe

**asylum** (uh-SYE-lum)—a hospital for people who are mentally ill and cannot live by themselves

**brute** (BROOT)—a rough or violent person

**detonate** (DET-uh-nate)—to set off an explosion

**projectile** (pruh-JEK-tuhl)—an object, such as a bullet or missile, that is thrown or shot through the air

**pummel** (PUHM-uhl)—to punch someone or something repeatedly

**ransom** (RAN-suhm)—money that is being demanded before someone who is being held captive is set free

**silhouette** (sil-oo-ET)—a dark outline seen against a light background

**Utility Belt** (yoo-TIL-uh-tee BELT)—Batman's belt, which holds all of his weaponry and gadgets

# BANE

**Real Name:**
**Unknown**

**Occupation:**
**Assassin and**
**Professional Criminal**

**Base:**
**Gotham City**

**Height:**
**6 feet 8 inches**

**Weight:**
**350 lbs.**

**Eyes:**
**Brown**

**Hair:**
**Brown**

Bane's background is a mystery, even to Batman. The only thing known for sure is that Bane was once a prisoner. He was chosen as a test subject for a new drug called Venom. The drug gave Bane superhuman strength. He now uses it to stay strong and works as one of Gotham City's criminal masterminds. Bane's greatest desire is to be the one person who can defeat the Dark Knight — permanently.

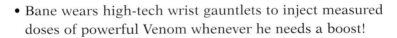

- Bane wears high-tech wrist gauntlets to inject measured doses of powerful Venom whenever he needs a boost!

- The hulking super-villain is equal parts brawn and brains, making him a formidable foe for the Dark Knight.

- Bane spent most of his childhood in Santa Prisca's Peña Duro prison. While there, his only friend became a stuffed teddy bear name Osoito, given to him by a rare Catholic missionary.

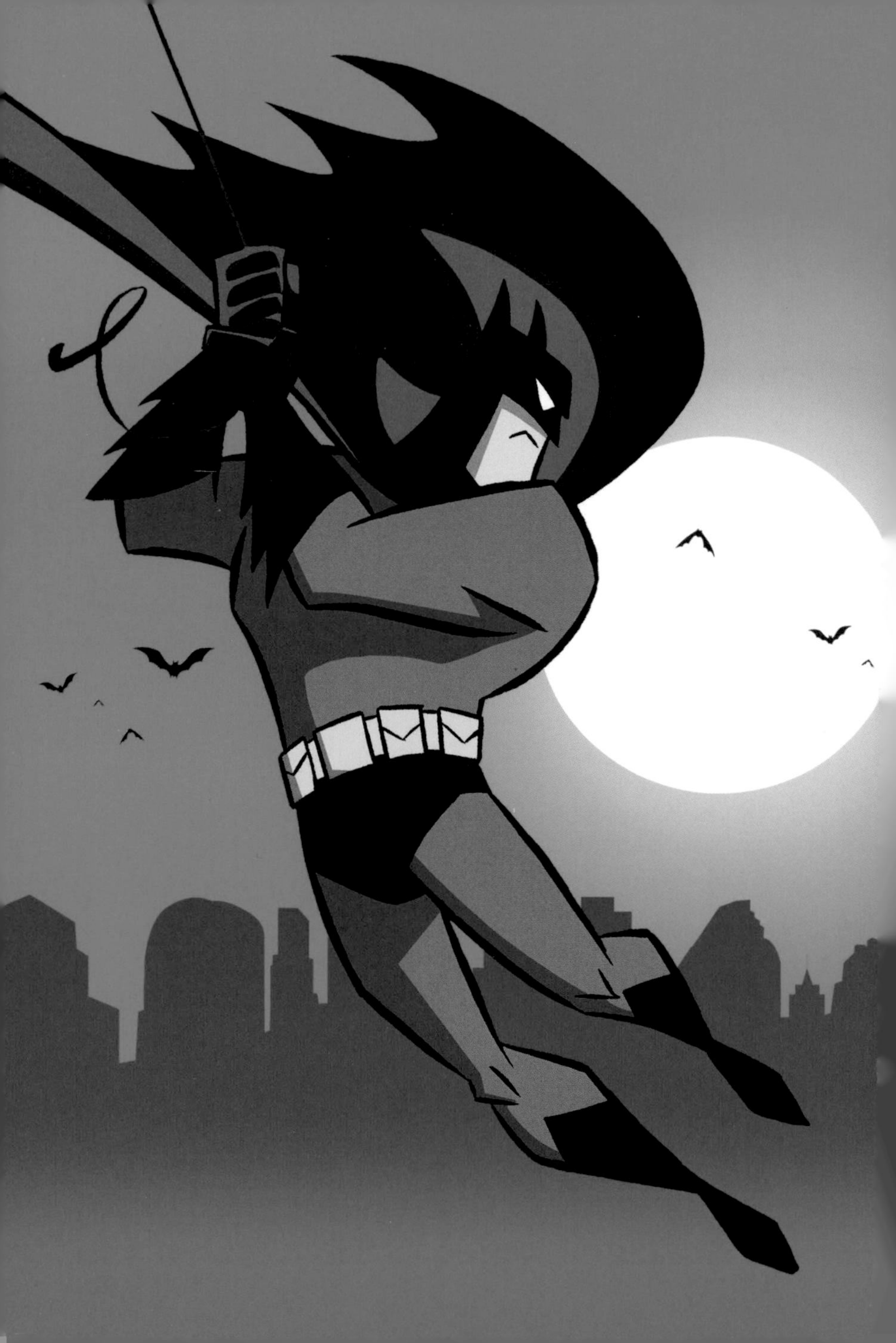